"Is that the question you wanted to ask me?"

Tarek laughed at that, as if it was funny. And Anya took the opportunity to ask herself what she was doing here. Why wasn't she on her way to the American embassy right now?

Why was she sitting here next to Tarek, imprisoning herself by choice, as if he was cupping her between his palms?

Worse still, she had the distinct sensation that he knew it.

"It is more a proposition than a question," he told her.

And Anya did not need to let that word kick around inside her, leaving trails of dangerous sparks behind. But she didn't do a thing to stop it. "Do you often proposition your former captives?"

"Not quite like this, Doctor." He didn't smile then, though she thought his eyes gleamed. And she felt the molten heat of it, the wild flame. She thought she saw stars again, but it was only Tarek, gazing back at her. "I want you to marry me."

USA TODAY bestselling and RITA® Award–nominated author **Caitlin Crews** loves writing romance. She teaches her favorite romance novels in creative-writing classes at places like UCLA Extension's prestigious Writers' Program, where she finally gets to utilize the MA and PhD in English literature she received from the University of York in England. She currently lives in the Pacific Northwest with her very own hero and too many pets. Visit her at caitlincrews.com.

Books by Caitlin Crews

Harlequin Presents

Once Upon a Temptation

Claimed in the Italian's Castle

One Night With Consequences

The Italian's Twin Consequences
His Two Royal Secrets
Secrets of His Forbidden Cinderella

Passion in Paradise

The Italian's Pregnant Cinderella

Royal Christmas Weddings

Christmas in the King's Bed
His Scandalous Christmas Princess

Secret Heirs of Billionaires

Unwrapping the Innocent's Secret

Visit the Author Profile page
at Harlequin.com for more titles.

Caitlin Crews

CHOSEN FOR HIS DESERT THRONE

HARLEQUIN®
PRESENTS®

Recycling programs
for this product may
not exist in your area.

ISBN-13: 978-1-335-40377-3

Chosen for His Desert Throne

Copyright © 2020 by Caitlin Crews

For questions and comments about the quality of this book,
please contact us at CustomerService@Harlequin.com.

Harlequin Enterprises ULC
22 Adelaide St. West, 40th Floor
Toronto, Ontario M5H 4E3, Canada
www.Harlequin.com

Printed in U.S.A.

CHOSEN FOR HIS
DESERT THRONE

For Eileen, of course.

CHAPTER ONE

SHEIKH TAREK BIN ALZALAM had accomplished a remarkable amount in his first year as undisputed ruler of his small, mighty country.

He had accomplished more than he'd lost.

This was not only his opinion, he thought as he greeted the one-year anniversary of his father's death. It was fact, law, and would become legend.

He stood at the window of the royal bedchamber, gazing out on the ancient, prosperous walled capital city that was now his own. The city—and the desert beyond—that he had fought so hard for.

That he would always fight for, he asserted to himself as the newly risen desert sun bathed his naked body in its light, playing over the scars he bore from this past year of unrest. The scars he would always wear as they faded from red wounds to white badges of honor—the physical manifestation of what he was willing to do for his people.

His father's death had been sad, if not unexpected after his long illness, twelve months ago. Tarek was his eldest son and had been groomed since birth to step into power. He had grieved the loss of his father as a good son should, but he had been ready to take his rightful place at the head of the kingdom.

But his brother Rafiq had let his ambition get the best of him. Tarek hadn't seen the danger until it was too late—and it was his younger brother's bloody attempt to grab power no matter the cost that had required Tarek to begin his reign as more warrior than King. In the tradition of those who had carved this kingdom from the mighty desert centuries ago, one rebellion after another.

Or so he told himself. Because his was not the only brother in the history of this kingdom who had turned treacherous. There was something about being close to the throne yet never destined to rule that drove some men mad.

As King, he could almost understand it.

As a brother, he would never understand it—but he rarely allowed himself to think of that darkness. That betrayal.

Because nothing could come of it, save pain.

His mother had always told him that love was for the weak. Tarek would not make that mistake again. Ever. His blind love for Rafiq had nearly cost him the kingdom.

And his life.

But now his brother's misguided and petty revolution was over. Tarek's rule was both established and accepted across the land—celebrated, even—

and he chose to think of the past year's turmoil as more good than bad.

Some rulers never had the opportunity to prove to their people who they were.

Tarek, by contrast, had introduced himself to his subjects. With distinction.

He had shown them his judgment and his mercy in one, for he had not cut down his younger brother when he could have. And when he knew full well—little as he wished to know such things—that had Rafiq accomplished his dirty little coup he would have hung Tarek's body from the highest minaret in the capital city and let it rot.

Tarek could have reacted with all the passion and anguish that had howled within him, but he preferred to play a longer game. He was a king, not a child.

He had made Rafiq's trial swift and public. He'd wanted the whole of the kingdom to watch and tally up for themselves his once beloved brother's many crimes against Tarek—and more important, against them. He had not taken out his feelings of betrayal on his brother, though that, too, would have been seen as a perfectly reasonable response to the kind of treachery Rafiq had attempted.

His brother had tried to kill him, yet lived.

Rafiq had been remanded to a jail cell, not the executioners block.

"*Behold my mercy,*" Tarek had said to him on the day of his sentencing. There in the highest court of the land, staring at his younger brother but seeing the traitor. Or trying to see nothing but the traitor his younger brother had become. "*I do not require your blood, brother. Only your penance.*"

The papers had run with it. A Bright and New Day Has Dawned in the Kingdom! they'd cried, and now, standing in the cleansing, pure heat of the desert's newest sun, Tarek finally felt as if he, too, was bright straight through.

Now the dust was settled. His brother's mess had been well and truly handled, cleaned away, and countered. It was time to set down sword and war machine alike and turn his thoughts toward more domestic matters.

And while you're at it, think no more of what has been lost, he ordered himself.

He sighed a bit as he turned from the embrace of the sun. He did not need to look at all the portraits on his walls, particularly in the various salons that made up his royal apartments. Kings stretching back to medieval times, warlords and tyrants, beloved rulers and local saints alike. What all those men had in common with Tarek, aside from their blood, was that their domestic matters had dynastic implications.

If Tarek had no issue and his brother's co-conspirators rose again, and this time managed to succeed in an assassination attempt, Rafiq could call himself the rightful King of Alzalam. Many would agree.

It was time to marry.

Like it or not.

After his usual morning routine, Tarek made his

way through the halls of the palace. The royal seat of Alzalam's royal family was a sixteenth-century showpiece that generations of his ancestors had tended to, lavishing more love upon the timeless elegance of the place than they ever had upon their wives or children.

"The palace is a symbol of what can be," his wise father had told him long ago. *"It is aspirational. You must never forget that at best, the King should be, too."*

Tarek was not as transported by architecture as some of his blood had been in the past but he, too, took pride in the great palace that spoke not only of Alzalam's military might, but the artistic passion of its people. Like many countries in the region, packed tight on the Arabian Peninsula, his people were a mix of desert tribesmen and canny oil profiteers. His people craved their old ways even as they embraced the new, and Tarek understood that his role was to be the bridge between the two.

His father had prepared him. And before his death, the old King had arranged a sensible marriage for his son and heir that would allow Tarek to best lead the people into a future that would have to connect desert and oil, past and present.

Tarek tried and failed to pull to his mind details of his bride-to-be as he crossed the legendary central courtyard, a soothing oasis in the middle of the palace, and headed toward his offices. Where he daily left behind the fairy-tale King and was instead the

London School of Economics educated CEO of this country. He could not have said which role he valued more, but he could admit, as the courtyard performed its usual magic in him, that he was pleased he could finally set aside the other role that had claimed the bulk of his attention this last year. That of warlord and general.

Everything was finally as he wished it. There had been no unrest in the kingdom since his brother had surrendered. And with him locked away at last, the kingdom could once again enjoy its prosperity. No war, no civil unrest, no reason at all not to start concentrating on making his own heirs. The more the better.

He inclined his head as he passed members of his staff, all of whom either stood at attention or bowed low at the sight of him. But he smiled at his senior aide as he entered his office suite, because Ahmed had not only proved his loyalty to the crown repeatedly in the last year—he had made it more than clear that he supported Tarek personally, too.

"Good morning, Sire," Ahmed said, executing a low bow. "The kingdom wakes peaceful today. All is well."

"I'm happy to hear it." Tarek paused as he accepted the stack of messages his aide handed him. "Ahmed, I think the time has come."

"The time, Sire?"

Tarek nodded, the decision made. "Invite my betrothed's father to wait attendance upon me this afternoon. I'm ready to make the settlements."

"As you wish, Sire," Ahmed murmured, bowing his way out of the room.

Tarek could have sworn his typically unflappable aide looked…apprehensive. He couldn't think why.

Again, Tarek tried to recall the girl in question. He knew he had known them once—if only briefly. His father had presented him with a number of choices and he had a vague memory of a certain turn of cheek—then again, perhaps that had been one of his mistresses. His father had died not long after, Rafiq had attempted his coup, and Tarek had not allowed himself the distraction of women in a long while.

It was a measure of how calm things were that he allowed it now.

Tarek tossed the stack of messages onto the imposing desk that had taken up the better part of one side of the royal office for as long as he could remember. He crossed instead to the wall of glass before him, sweeping windows and arched doors that led out to what was known as the King's Overlook. It was an ancient balcony that allowed him to look down over his beloved fortress of a city yet again. These stones raised up from sand that his family had always protected and ever would.

He nodded, pleased.

For he would raise sons here. He would hold each one aloft, here where his father had held him, and show them what mattered. The people, the walls. The desert sun and the insistent sands. He would teach them to be good men, better rulers, excellent businessmen, and great warriors.

He would teach them, first and foremost, how to be brothers who would protect each other—not rise up against each other.

If he had to produce thirty sons himself to make certain the kingdom remained peaceful, he would do it.

"So I vow," he said then, out loud, to the watching, waiting desert. To the kingdom at his feet that he served more than he ruled, and ever would. "So it shall be."

But later that day he stared at the man who was meant to become his father-in-law before him without comprehension.

"Say that again," he suggested, sitting behind his desk as if the chair was its own throne. No doubt with an expression on his face to match his lack of comprehension. "I cannot believe I heard you correctly."

This was no servant who stood across from him. Mahmoud Al Jazeer was one of the richest men in the kingdom, from an ancient line that had once held royal aspirations. Tarek's own father had considered the man a close, personal friend.

It was very unlikely that the man had ever bent a knee to anyone, but here, today, he wrung his hands. And folded himself in half, assuming a servile position that would have been astounding—even amusing—in any other circumstances.

Had not what Mahmoud just told his King been impossible.

On every level.

"I cannot explain this turn of events, Sire," the older man said, his voice perilously close to a wail—also astonishing. "I am humiliated. My family will bear the black mark of this shame forever. But I cannot pretend it has not happened."

Tarek sat back in his chair, studying Mahmoud. And letting the insult of what the other man had confessed sit there between them, unadorned.

"What you are telling me is that you have no control over your own family," he said with a soft menace. "No ability to keep the promises you made yourself. You are proclaiming aloud that your word is worthless. Is that what you are telling your King?"

The other man looked ill. "Nabeeha has always been a headstrong girl. I must confess that I spoiled her all her life, as her mother has long been the favorite of all my wives. My sons warned me of this danger, but I did not listen. The fault is mine."

"The betrothal was agreed upon," Tarek reminded him. "Vows were made and witnessed while my father yet lived."

He remembered the signing of all those documents, here in this very room. His father, already weak, had been thrilled that his son's future was settled. Mahmoud had been delighted that he would take a place of even greater prominence in the kingdom. But it had taken Ahmed's presentation of the dossier the palace kept on the woman who was to be his Queen to refresh his recollection of the girl in question, who had not been present that day, as it was not her signature that mattered.

Perhaps that had been an oversight.

"I would have her keep those vows," Mahmoud said hurriedly. "She was only meant to get an education. A little bit of polish, the better to acquit herself on your arm, Sire. That was the only reason I agreed to let her go overseas. It was all in service to your greater glory."

"Those are pretty words, but they are only words. Meanwhile, my betrothed is…what? At large in North America? Never to be heard from again?"

"I am humiliated by her actions," Mahmoud cried, and this time, it was definitely a wail. And well he should wail, Tarek thought. For his daughter's defection was not only an embarrassment—it would cost his family dear. "But she has asked for asylum in Canada. And worse, received it."

"This gets better and better." Tarek shook his head, and even laughed, though the sound seemed to hit the other man like a bullet. "On what grounds does the pampered daughter of an international businessman, fiancée of a king, seek asylum?"

"I cannot possibly understand the workings of the Western governments," the man hedged. "Can anyone?"

Tarek's mouth curved. It was not a smile. "You do understand that I betrothed myself to your daughter as a favor to my father. An acknowledgment of the friendship he shared with you. But you and I? We do not share this same bond. And if your daughter does not respect it…"

He shrugged. The other man quailed and shook.

"Sire, I beg of you…"

"If your daughter does not wish to marry her King, I will not force her." Tarek kept his gaze on his father's friend, and did not attempt to soften his tone. "I will find a girl with gratitude for the honor being done her, Mahmoud. Your daughter is welcome to enjoy her asylum as she sees fit."

Despite the increased wailing that occurred then, Tarek dismissed the older man before he was tempted to indulge his own sense of insult further.

"*You must take the part of the kingdom*," his father had always cautioned him. "*Your own feelings cannot matter when the country hangs in the balance.*"

He reminded himself of that as he looked at the photograph before him of the blandly smiling girl, a stranger to him, who had so disliked the notion of marrying him that she had thrown herself on the mercy of a foreign government. What was he to make of that?

Then, with a single barked command, he summoned Ahmed before him.

"Why have I not been made aware that the woman who was to become my bride has sought, and apparently received, political asylum in a foreign country?"

Ahmed did not dissemble. It was one reason Tarek trusted him. "It was a developing situation we hoped to solve, Sire. Preferably before you knew of it."

"Am I such an ineffectual monarch that I am to be kept in the dark about my own kingdom?" Tarek asked, his voice quiet.

Lethal.

"We hoped to resolve the situation," Ahmed said calmly. No wailing. No shaking. "There was no wish to deceive and, if you do not mind my saying so, you had matters of far greater importance weighing upon you this last year. What was a tantrum of a spoiled girl next to an attempted coup?"

Tarek could see the truth in that. His sense of insult faded. "And can you explain to me, as her father could not, why it is that the girl would be granted political asylum in the first place? She was allowed to leave the kingdom to pursue her studies. Supported entirely by me and my government. She would face no reprisals of any kind were she to return. How does she qualify?"

Ahmed straightened, which was not a good sign. "I believe that there are some factions in the West who feel that you have…violated certain laws."

Tarek arched a brow. "I make the laws and therefore, by definition, cannot violate them."

"Not your laws, Sire." Ahmed bowed slightly, another warning. "There are allegations of human rights abuses."

"Against me?" Tarek was genuinely surprised. "They must mean my brother, surely."

He did try not to speak his brother's name. Not thinking it was more difficult.

"No, the complaint is against you. Your government, not his attempt at one."

"I had the option for capital punishment," Tarek argued. "I chose instead to demonstrate benevolence. Was this not clear?"

"It does not concern your brother or his treatment." Ahmed met Tarek's gaze, and held it. "It is about the doctors."

He might as well have said, *the unicorns.*

Tarek blinked. "I beg your pardon?"

"The doctors, Sire. They were picked up eight months ago after an illegal border crossing in the north."

"What sort of doctors?" But even as Tarek asked, a vague memory reasserted itself. "Wait. I remember now. It is that aid organization, isn't it? Traveling doctors, moving about from one war zone to another."

"They are viewed as heroes."

Tarek sighed. "Release these heroes, then. Why is this an issue?"

"The male doctors were released once you reclaimed your throne," Ahmed said without inflection, another one of his strengths. "As were all the political prisoners, according to your orders at the time. But there was one female doctor in the group.

And because she was a Western woman, and because there are no facilities for female prisoners in the capital city, she was placed in the dungeon."

Tarek found himself sitting forward. "The dungeon. *My* dungeon? Here in the palace?"

"Yes, sire." Ahmed inclined his head. "And as you are aware, I am sure, prisoners cannot be released from the palace dungeons except by your personal decree."

Tarek slowly climbed to his feet, his blood pumping through him as if he found himself in another battle. Much like the ones he had fought in his own halls on that bloody night Rafiq and his men had come. The ones he wore still on his body and always would.

"Ahmed." The lash of his voice would have felled a lesser man, but Ahmed stood tall. "Am I to understand that after the lengths I went to, to show the world that I am a merciful and just ruler of this kingdom…this whole time, there has been not merely a Western woman locked beneath my feet, but a *doctor*? A do-gooder who roams the planet, healing others as she goes?"

Ahmed nodded. "I am afraid so."

"I might as well have locked up a saint. No wonder an otherwise pointless girl, who should have considered herself lucky to be chosen as my bride, has instead thrown herself on the tender mercies of the Canadians. I am tempted to do the same."

"It was an oversight, Sire. Nothing more. There

was so much upheaval. And then the trial. And then, I think, it was assumed that you were pleased to keep things as they were."

The worst part was that Tarek could blame no one but himself, much as he might have liked to. This was his kingdom. His palace, his prisoners. He might not have ordered the woman jailed, but he hadn't asked after the status of any state prisoners, had he?

He would not make that mistake again. He could feel the scars on his body, throbbing as if they were new. This was on him.

Tarek did not waste any more time talking. He set off through the palace again, grimly this time. He bypassed graceful halls of marble and delicate, filigreed details enhancing each and every archway. He crossed the main courtyard and then the smaller, more private one. This one a pageant of flowers, the next symphony of fountains.

He marched through to the oldest part of the palace, the medieval keep. And the ancient dungeons that had been built beneath it by men long dead and gone.

The guards standing at the huge main door did double takes that would have been comical had Tarek been in a lighter mood. They leaped aside, flinging open the iron doors, and Tarek strode within. He was aware that not only Ahmed, but a parade of staff scurried behind him, as if clinging to the hem of his robes that towed them all along with the force of his displeasure.

He had played in these dungeons as a child, though it had been expressly forbidden by his various tutors. But there had never been any actual prisoners here in his lifetime. The dungeons were a threat, nothing more. The bogeyman the adults in his life had trotted out to convince a headstrong child to behave.

Tarek expected to find them dark and grim, like something out of an old movie.

But it turned out there were lights. An upgrade from torches set in the thick walls, but it was still a place of grim stone and despair. His temper pounded through him as he walked ancient halls he hadn't visited since he was a child. He tried to look at this from all angles, determined to figure out a way to play this public relations disaster to his advantage.

Before he worried about that, however, he would have to tend to the prisoner herself. See her pampered, cared for, made well again. And he had no idea what he would find.

It occurred to him to wonder, for the first time, what it was his guards did in his name.

"Where is she?" he growled at the man in uniform who rushed to bow before him, clearly the head of this dungeon guard he hadn't known he possessed.

"She is in the Queen's Cell," the man replied.

The Queen's Cell. So named for the treacherous wife of an ancient king who had been too prominent to execute. The King she had betrayed had built her a cell of her very own down here in these cold, dark stones. Tarek's memory of it was the same stone walls and iron bars as any other cell, but fitted with a great many tightly barred windows, too.

So she could look out and mourn the world she would never be a part of again.

This was where he—for it was his responsibility and no matter that he hadn't known—had locked away a Western *doctor,* God help him.

But Tarek had been fighting more dangerous battles for a year. He did not waste time girding his loins. He dove in. He rounded the last corner and marched himself up to the mouth of the cell.

And then stopped dead.

Because the human misery he had been expecting…wasn't on display.

The cell was no longer bare and imposing, the way it was in Tarek's memory. There was a rug on the floor. Books on shelves that newly-lined the walls. And the bed—a cot in place of a pallet on the stone floor—was piled high with linens. Perhaps not the finest linens he'd ever beheld, but clearly there with an eye toward comfort.

And curled up on the bed—neither in chains nor in a broken heap on the floor—was a woman.

She wore a long tunic and pants, a typical outfit for a local woman, and the garments did not look ragged or torn. They were loose, but clean. Her dark hair was long and fell about her shoulders, but it too looked perfectly clean and even brushed. She was lean, but not the sort of skinny that would indicate she'd been in any way malnourished. And try as he might, Tarek could not see a single bruise or injury.

He assessed the whole of her, twice, then found her eyes.

They were dark and clever. A bit astonished, he thought, but the longer she stared back at him, the less he was tempted to imagine it was the awe he usually inspired. And the longer he gazed at her, the more he noticed more things about her than simply the welfare of her body.

Like the fact she was young. Much younger than he'd imagined, he realized. He'd expected to find an older woman who suited the image of a *doctor* in his head. Gray-haired, lined cheeks… But this doctor not only showed no obvious signs of mistreatment, she was…

Pretty.

"You look important," the woman said, shocking Tarek by using his native tongue.

"I expected you to speak English," he replied, in the same language, though Ahmed had only said she was Western, not English speaking. She could have been French. German. Spanish.

"We can do that," she replied. And she was still lounging there on the bed, whatever book she'd been reading still open before her as if he was an annoyance, nothing more. It took Tarek a moment, once he got past the insolent tone, to realize she'd switched languages. And was American. "You don't really look like a prison guard. Too shiny."

Tarek knew that his staff had filed in behind him at the shocked sounds they all made. He lifted a finger, and there was silence.

And he watched as the woman tracked that, smirked, and then raised her gaze to his again. As if they were equals.

"Important *and* you have a magic finger," she said.

Tarek was not accustomed to insolence. From anyone—and certainly not from women, who spent the better part of any time in his presence attempting to curry his favor, by whatever means available to them.

He waited, but this woman only gazed back at him, expectantly.

As if he was here to wait upon her.

He reminded himself, grudgingly, that he was. That he had not fought a war, against his own brother, so that the world could sit back and judge him harshly.

At least not for things he had not done deliberately.

"I am Tarek bin Alzalam," he informed her, as behind him, all the men bowed their heads in appropriate deference. The woman did not. He continued, then. "I am the ruler of this kingdom."

The doctor blinked, but if that was deference, it was insufficient. And gone in a flash. "You're the Sheikh?"

"I am."

She sat up then, pushing her hair back from her

face, though she did not rise fully from her bed. Nor fall to her knees before him, her mouth alive with songs of praise.

In point of fact, she smirked again. And her eyes flashed.

"I've been waiting to meet you for eight long months," she said, the slap of her voice so disrespectful it made Tarek's eyes widen.

Around him, his men made audible noises of dismay.

Once again, he quieted them. Once again, she tracked the movement of his finger and looked upon him with insolence.

"And so you have," Tarek gritted out.

There was still no sign of deference. No hint that she might wish to plead for her freedom.

"I'm Dr. Anya Turner, emergency medicine." Again, her dark eyes flashed. "I'm a doctor. I help people. While you're nothing but a tiny little man who thinks his dungeon and his armed guards make him something other than a pig."

CHAPTER TWO

ANYA HAD EXPECTED this moment to be sweet and satisfying, if it ever came, but it went off better than she'd imagined.

And she'd done very little else *but* imagine it.

For months.

The Sheikh of Alzalam himself stood before her. The man who every guard she'd encountered had spoken of in terms of such overwrought awe and glory that they'd made it a certainty that Anya would have loathed him on sight.

Even if she wasn't incarcerated in his personal prison.

She didn't much care for arrogant men at the best of times, which this obviously was not. Between her own father and every male doctor she'd ever met— not to mention the surgeons, who could teach arrogance to kings like this one and would not need an invitation to do so—Anya was full up on condescending males. An eight-month holiday in the company of these prison guards had not helped any.

And the way the Sheikh stared back at her, as if *dumbstruck* that she wasn't even now weeping at his feet, did not exactly inspire her to change her mind about the male ego.

The stunned silence went on.

Anya found herself sitting a little straighter, a little taller, as if that would protect her if the Sheikh had finally turned up only to go medieval on her. It occurred to her that, perhaps, she should have tried to get herself out of the dungeon before shooting off her mouth.

A lesson she never seemed to learn, did she?

After all these months, she'd figured she already knew how bad things could get here. She'd decided that sharing her unbridled feelings couldn't make things *worse*. What was worse than finding herself locked away in a literal dungeon in a country she wasn't even supposed to be in—separated from her colleagues who were very possibly dead and being kept alive for reasons no one had seen fit to share with her?

But as she stared back at the tall, ferocious, and obviously powerful man on the other side of her cell door, she was terribly afraid he might have a few answers to that question she wouldn't like.

Anya held her breath, but he didn't move. He only stared her down, inviting her to do the same.

There was a wall of other men behind him, staring at her in shock and disapproval, but *he* looked like he was attempting to crawl inside her head.

Anya didn't know what was wrong with her that she wanted to let him. Just because staring at him made her feel alive again. Just because it was different.

It had been *eight months*. Some two hundred and forty days, give or take. At first she'd intended to scratch each day into the walls, because wasn't that what people did? But she'd quickly discovered that someone—quite a few someones, or so she hoped, given the number of slash marks she'd found—had beaten her to it. She'd found that depressing. So depressing that she'd covered up the marks once the guards started permitting her furniture.

She had already cycled through fear. Despair. Over and over again, in those early days, until the panic faded.

Because that was the funny thing about time. It had a flattening effect. The human body couldn't maintain adrenaline that long. Sooner or later, routine took over. And with routine, a tacit acceptance.

She'd become friendly with her guards, though never *too* friendly. She'd learned the language, because that meant she was less in the dark. They'd made her comfortable, and over time, it became more and more clear that they had no intention of hurting her. Or no immediate plans to try, anyway.

Anya would have said she didn't have much fear left. She would have meant it.

Though the longer she stared at the man before her, stern and forbidding and focused intently on her, the more it reintroduced itself to the back of her neck. Then began tracing its way down her spine.

Maybe that's not entirely fear, something inside her suggested.

But she dismissed that. Because it was crazy.

And she had no intention of losing her mind in here, no matter how tempting it was. No matter how much she thought she might like a little touch of oblivion to make the time pass.

Okay, yes, she told herself impatiently. *He is remarkably attractive for a pig.*

Though *attractive* was an understatement.

He was dressed all in white, and in a contrast to the variously colored robes all the men wore around him, his fit him more closely. And more, were edged in gold. She probably should have known from that alone that he was the man in charge.

Sheikh. Ruler. King. Whatever they called him, he looked like the love child of the desert sun and some sort of bird of prey. A falcon, maybe, cast in bronze and inhabiting the big, brawny body of an extraordinarily fit man.

She was holding her breath again, but it was different. It was—

Stop it, Anya ordered herself.

This was no time to pay attention to something as altogether pointless as how physically fit the man was. So what if he had wide shoulders and narrow hips, all of it made of muscle. So what if he made gilt-edged robes look better than three-piece suits.

What mattered was that he'd thrown her into his dungeon and, as far she could tell, had thrown away the key, too. Anya had done a lot of dumb things in her lifetime—from allowing her father to bully her into medical school to focusing on emergency medicine because he'd told she was unsuited for it, to accepting the job that had brought her here, mostly to escape the job she'd left behind in Houston—but surely sudden-onset Stockholm syndrome would catapult her straight past dumb into unpardonably stupid.

She was sure she saw temper glitter in his dark, dark eyes. She would have sworn that same temper made that muscle in his jaw flex.

She *did not* feel an echo of those things inside. She refused to feel a thing.

"Please accept my humblest apologies," he said, and now that she wasn't gearing up to tell him what she thought of him, there was no escaping the richness of his voice. He spoke English with a British intonation, and she told herself it was adrenaline that raced through her, then. She'd forgotten what it felt like, that was all. "There has been great unrest in the kingdom. It is unfortunate that your presence here was not made known to me until now."

That was not at all what Anya had been expecting.

It felt a lot as if she'd flung herself against the walls—something she had, in fact, done repeatedly in the early days—only to find instead of the expected stone and pitiless bars, there was nothing but paper. She suddenly felt as if she was teetering on the edge of a sharp, steep cliff, arms pinwheeling as she fought to find her balance.

Something knotted up in her solar plexus.

It was a familiar knot, to her dismay. That same knot had been her constant companion and her greatest enemy over the last few years. It had grown bigger and thornier as she'd grown increasingly less capable of managing her own stress.

When here she'd been all of five minutes ago, feeling something like self-congratulatory that no matter what else was happening—or not happening, as was the case with whiling away a life behind bars—she was no longer one panic attack away from the embarrassing end of her medical career.

Thinking of her medical career made that knot swell. She rubbed at it, then wished she hadn't, because the Sheikh's dark gaze dropped to her hand. A lot like he thought she was touching herself *for* him.

Which made that prickle of sensation tracing its way down her spine seem to bloom. Into something Anya couldn't quite convince herself was fear.

"Are you apologizing for putting me in your dungeon or for *forgetting* you put me in your dungeon?" she asked, a little more forcefully than she'd intended. But she lifted her chin, straightened her shoulders, and went with it. "And regardless of which it is, do you really think eight months of imprisonment is something an apology can fix?"

He shifted slightly, barely inclining his head at the

man beside him, who Anya knew was in charge of these dungeons. As the round little toad had pompously informed her of that fact, repeatedly. And she watched, astonished, as the keys were produced immediately, her cell was unlocked, and then the door flung wide.

The Sheikh inclined his head again. This time at her.

"I can only apologize again for your ordeal," he said in that low voice of his that made her far too aware of how powerful he was. Because it *hummed* in her. "I invite you to leave this prison behind and become, instead, my honored guest."

Anya didn't move. Not even a muscle. She eyed the obvious predator before her as if, should she breathe too loudly, he might attack in all that ivory and gold. "Is there a difference?"

The man before her did not shout. She could see temper and arrogance in his gaze, but he did not give in to them. Though there were men all around him, many of them scowling at her as if she was nothing short of appalling, he did not do the same.

Instead, he held her gaze, and she could not have said what it was about him that made something in her quiver. Why she felt, suddenly, as if she could tip forward off of that cliff, fall and fall and fall, and never reach the depths of his dark eyes.

Then, clearly to the astonishment and bewilderment of the phalanx of men around him, Sheikh Tarek bin Alzalam held out his hand.

"Come," he said again, an intense urging. "You will be safe. You have my word."

And later, Anya would have no idea why that worked. Why she should take the word of a strange man whose fault it was, whether he'd known it or not, that she'd been locked away for eight long months.

Maybe it was as simple as the fact that he was beautiful. Not the way the men back home were sometimes, mousse in their hair and their T-shirt sleeves rolled *just so*. But in the same stark and over-whelming way the city outside these windows was, a gold stone fortress that was, nonetheless, impossibly beautiful. Desert sunrises and sunsets. The achingly beautiful blue sky. The songs that hung over the city sometimes, bringing her to tears.

He was harsh and stern and still, the only word that echoed inside her wasn't *pig*. It was *beautiful*.

Anya didn't have it in her to resist.

Not after nearly three seasons of cold stone and iron bars.

Before she could think better of it—or talk herself out of it—she rose. She crossed the floor of her cell as if his gaze was a tractor beam and she was unable to fight it. As if she was his to command.

Almost without meaning to, she slipped her hand into his.

Heat punched into her as his fingers closed over hers. Anya was surprised to find them hard and faintly rough, as if this man—this King—regularly performed some kind of actual labor that left calluses there.

Snips of overheard conversations between guards echoed inside her, then. Tales of a king who had risen from his bed and held off the enemy with his own two hands and an ancient sword, like something out of a myth.

Surely not, Anya thought.

She saw a flicker of something in his dark eyes, then. That same heat that should have embarrassed her, yes, but something else, too.

Maybe it was surprise that there was this *storm* between them, as if a simple touch could change the weather.

Indoors.

You have been locked up too long, Anya snapped at herself.

He did something with his head that was not a bow of any kind, but made her think of a deep, formal bow all the same.

Then, still gripping her hand and holding it out before him—like something out of an old storybook, wholly heedless of the way sensation lashed at her like rain—the King led her out of the dungeon.

And despite herself—despite every furious story she'd told herself over the past months, every scenario she'd imagined and reimagined in her head— as they emerged from the steep stone steps into what was clearly the main part of the palace, Anya was charmed.

She told herself it was as simple as moving from darkness into light. Anyone would be dazzled, she assured herself, after so many months below ground. Especially when she'd been brought here that terrifying night they'd been captured, hustled through lines of scary men with weapons, certain that the fact she'd been separated from her colleagues meant only terrible things.

Today Anya still had no idea what she was walking into, but at least it was pretty.

More than pretty. Everything seemed to be made of marble or mosaic, inlaid with gold and precious stones or carved into glorious patterns. It was all gleaming white or the sparkling blue water of the fountains. There were splashes of color, exultant flowers, and the impossibly blue sky there above her in wide-open courtyards, like a gift.

She found herself tipping back her face to let the sun move over it, even though she knew that gave too much away. That it made her much too vulnerable.

But if he was only taking her from one cell to another, she intended to enjoy it.

Anya had learned the language, but still, she didn't understand what Tarek muttered to a specific man who strode directly behind him. The rest of the men fell away. There were more impossibly graceful halls, statues and art that made a deep, old longing inside her swell into being, and then this blade of a king led her into a room so dizzy with light that she found herself blinking as she looked around.

The light bounced off all the surfaces, gleaming so hard it almost hurt, but Anya loved it. Even when her eyes teared up, she loved it.

Tarek dropped her hand, then beckoned for her to take a seat in one of the low couches she belatedly realized formed a circle in the center of the room. But how could she notice the brightly patterned cushions and seats when the walls were encrusted in jewels and the room opened up on to a long, white terrace? She thought she saw the hint of a pool. And off to one side, more chairs, low tables, and lush green trees for shade.

"This is your suite and your salon," he told her. "I'm going to ask you some questions, and then I will leave you to reacclimate. You will be provided with whatever you need. Clothes to choose from, a bath with whatever accessories you require, and, of course, access to your loved ones using whatever medium you wish. My servants are even now assembling outside this room, ready to wait on you hand and foot. In the meantime, as I cannot imagine that the food in the dungeon speaks well of Alzalam and because I am afraid I must ask you these questions, I've taken the liberty of requesting a small tea service."

"A tea service," Anya repeated, and had to choke back the urge to burst out laughing. She coughed. "That is…the most insane and yet perfect thing you could possibly have said. *A tea service.*"

She suspected she was hysterical. Or about to be,

because she was clearly in shock and attempting to process it, when that was likely impossible. She was out of her cell, and that was what mattered. More, she did not think that Tarek had chosen this room bursting with light and open to the great outdoors by accident.

Yet somehow, she thought that after all of this, she might not survive if she broke apart like that. Here, now, when it seemed she might actually have made it through.

She would never forgive herself if she fell apart now.

When he was sitting opposite her, all his ivory and gold seeming a part of the light that she was suddenly bathed in. As if he was another jeweled thing, precious and impossible.

If she cried now, she would die.

And as if to taunt her, that knotted horror in her solar plexus pulled tight.

"You do not have to eat, of course," he said with a kind of matter-of-fact gentleness that made the knot ache and, lower, something deep in her belly begin to melt. "Nor am I suggesting that a few pastries can make up for what was done to you. Consider it the first of many gifts I intend to bestow upon you, as an apology for what has happened to you here."

Anya didn't really know how she was expected to respond to that. Because the fact was, she was still here and she couldn't quite believe what was happening. She shifted in her plush, soft seat and dug her fingernails into her thigh, hard. It hurt, but she didn't wake up to find herself in her cell. She'd had so many of those dreams at first, and still had them now and again. They were all so heartbreakingly realistic and every time, the shock of waking to find herself still stuck in that cell felt like the kind of blow she couldn't get up from.

Slowly, she released her painful grip on her own thigh and assessed her situation.

She hadn't been tossed on a truck headed for the border, or shot in the back of the head, or sent back to the States so she could throw herself off the plane to kiss the ground—not that she thought an airport floor would inspire her to do any such thing.

If this was truly freedom, or the start of it, she was still a long way off from having to sort through what remained of the life she'd left behind.

That was not a happy thought.

When the door swung open again, servants streamed inside bearing platters and pushing a cart. Her stomach rumbled at the sight. Plate after plate of delicacies were delivered to the low table between her and the King. Nuts and dates, the promised pastries, meats and spreads, breads and cheeses. Cakes and yogurts and what she thought was a take on baklava, drenched in a rich honey she could smell from where she sat. Bowls filled with savory dishes she couldn't identify, all of which looked beautiful and smelled even better. Pitchers of water, sparking and still. Tea in one silver carafe and in another, rich, dark coffee.

Anya might not trust her own happiness, or what was happening around her, but she could eat her fill for the first time in months, and for the moment that felt like the same thing. Because there were flavors again, as bright as the sun that careened around this room. Flavors and textures, each one a revelation, like colors on her tongue.

She glutted herself, happily, and didn't care if it made her sick.

While across from her, the Sheikh lounged in his seat and drank only coffee. Black.

Anya told herself there was no reason she should take that as some kind of warning.

When her belly was deliciously full, she sat back and took a very deep breath. And for the first time in a long while, Anya was aware of herself as a woman again. Not a prisoner. Not a doctor.

A woman, that was all, who had just engaged in the deeply sensual act of enjoying her food.

Perhaps it was because Tarek was so harshly, inarguably, a man. Here in the dizzy brightness and jeweled quiet of this room, there was no doubt in her mind that he was a king. Mythic or otherwise, and everything that entailed. It was the way he sat there, waiting for her—yet not precisely waiting. Because she could feel the power in him. It was unmistakable.

He filled the room, hotter than the sunshine that poured in from outside. Richer than the coffee and more intense than the sugar and butter, tartness and spice on her tongue.

And his gaze only seemed darker the longer he studied her.

Waiting her out, she understood then. Because he was in control, not her. Yet in a different way than her guards had been in control below, or the cell itself had contained her. Tarek did not need to place her behind bars.

Not when he could look at her and make her wonder why she couldn't stay right where she was, forever, if that would please him—

Get a grip, Anya, she ordered herself.

She'd thought him beautiful in the dungeons, but here, he was worse. Much worse. There was no getting away from the stark sensuality of his features, with that face like a hawk's that she wouldn't have been surprised to find stamped on old coins.

Anya felt distinctly grubby by comparison. She was suddenly entirely too aware that she had not had access to decent products in a long, long time. Her hair felt like straw. Her prison-issue clothes had suited her fine in the cell she'd eventually made, if not cozy, livable. But the gray drabness of the clothes she'd lived in for so long felt like an affront now. Here where this man watched her with an expression that, no matter what pretty words he spouted, did not strike her as remotely apologetic.

"You said you had questions for me," she said,

when it became clear to her that he was perfectly willing to sit there in silence. Watching her eat.

Making her feel as caged as if he held her between his hands.

It only made her feel more like a bedraggled piece of trash someone had flung onto his pristine marble floors. That, in turn, made her think of her long, quiet, painful childhood in her father's house. Her succession of stepmothers, each younger and prettier than the last.

Anya had never been a pretty girl. Not like her stepmothers. She'd never wanted to do the kind of work they did to remain so. And her father had always frowned and asked her why she would lower herself to worries about her appearance when she was supposedly intelligent, like him, thereby making certain Anya and the stepmother *du jour* were little better than enemies.

And sometimes a whole lot worse than that.

That didn't mean she wasn't aware of the ways she could use her appearance as a springboard toward confidence, upon occasion, when she wasn't feeling it internally. She didn't need a gown, or whatever it was the ladies wore in a place like this. But she wouldn't have minded a shower and some conditioner.

Still, he'd said he had his questions and Anya didn't know what would happen if she refused. Would it be straight back into the dungeon with her?

"Tell me how you came to be in my country," he

invited her, though she felt the truth of that invitation impress itself against her spine as the order it was. "In the middle of a minor revolution."

"Minor?"

The Sheikh did something with his chin that she might have called a shrug, had he been a lesser man. "Loss of life was minimal. My brother anticipated a quiet coup and was surprised when that was not what he got. He lives on in prison, an emblem to all of his own bad decisions and my mercy. Despite his best efforts, the country did not descend into chaos."

Anya didn't have a brother, but doubted she would sound so remote about a coup attempt if she did. "I guess you must not have been out there in the thick of it."

His lips thinned. "You are mistaken."

Anya blinked at that, and found herself clearing her throat. Unnecessarily. And more because of that storm in her than anything in her throat. A storm that wound around and around, then shifted into more of that melting that should have horrified her.

She told herself it was shock. This was all shock. Her whole body kept *reacting* to this man and she didn't like it, but it wasn't him.

You're not yourself, she told herself, but it didn't feel like an excuse.

It felt a lot more like permission.

But Anya had trained in emergency medicine. Then had trained more by flinging herself into the deep end, in and out of some of the worst places on the planet and usually with very little in the way of backup.

She could handle tea with a king, surely.

There were fewer bodily fluids, for one thing.

"Crossing into Alzalam was accidental," she told him. She'd gone over it a thousand times. Then a thousand more. "We were working in one of the refugee camps over the border. You know that civil war has been going on for a generation."

"Yes," the man across from her said quietly. "And it has ever been a horror."

As if he felt that horror deeply. Personally.

Her heart jolted, then thudded loudly.

"I'm surprised you think so," she said without thinking, and watched a royal eyebrow arch high on his ferociously stark brow. "That you are even aware of the scope of that kind of disaster from…" She glanced around. "Here."

"Because I am no different from a tyrant who rules by fear." His voice was soft, but she did not mistake the threat in it. "We are all the same, we desert men in our ancient kingdoms."

Her heart and that knot in her chest pulsed in concert, and she thought she might be shaking. God, she hoped she wasn't *shaking*, showing her weaknesses, letting him see how easily he intimidated her.

"To be fair," she managed to say, "my experience of desert kings has pretty much been nothing but death, disease, and dungeons. Not to discount the pastries, of course."

She was holding her breath again. His gaze was so dark, so merciless, that she was sure that if she dared look away—if she dared look down—she would find he'd made her into some of that filigree that lined his archways. An insubstantial lace, even if carved from bone.

And then, to her astonishment, the most dangerous man she'd ever met, who could lock her up for the rest of her life with a wave of one finger—or worse—

Smiled.

CHAPTER THREE

TAREK HAD NEVER before considered food erotic. It was fuel. It was sometimes a necessary evil. It could, upon occasion, be a form of communion.

But watching the doctor eat with abandon, as if every bite she put in her mouth was a new, sensual delight, was a revelation. She had him hard and ready. Intensely focused on her and the unbridled passion she displayed as if she was performing her joy for him alone.

He could not recall ever experiencing anything quite like it.

And certainly not because of a captive still in her prison attire.

Still, Tarek smiled at her as if none of this was happening. He reminded himself—perhaps a bit sternly—that honey attracted more bees than vinegar. And that even a king could allow himself to act sweet if it suited him. It helped that his plan of how to handle the world's reaction to her incarceration began to take form in his head.

But she did not look particularly pleased to receive

a smile from him. On the contrary, she looked…
poleaxed.

"Perhaps this is not the time to ask you these questions," he said after a moment, when she only stared
back at him. Her passionate eating on pause.

Tarek tried to let consideration and concern shine
forth from within him, and it wasn't entirely an act
for her benefit. He liked to think he was a compassionate man. Had he not proved it this dark year?
He was certainly the most compassionate King the
country had ever seen.

Surely the life he'd led had given him ample opportunity to practice.

Anya straightened her shoulders, a slight, deliberate jerk that he'd watched her do several times
now. As if she was snapping herself to attention. And
when she did, her brown eyes sharpened on him and
he wondered, idly enough, if this was the doctor in
her. That focus. That intensity.

That, too, made his sex heavy.

Later, Tarek promised himself, he would take a
moment to ask himself why, exactly, he found himself attracted to a prisoner only recently released
from his dungeon. Surely that spoke to issues within
himself he ought to resolve. Especially if he truly
thought himself compassionate in some way.

"I'm happy to answer questions now," she said,
with a certain bluntness that made Tarek blink.

He wondered if it was simply that she was a Western woman, doctor or no. They were different from

the women of his kingdom; he knew that already. Anya Turner was forthright, even so recently liberated from her prison cell. She appeared to have no trouble whatever meeting his gaze and more, holding it. The women of his country played far different games. They were masters of the soft sigh, the submissively lowered eyes, all to hide their warrior hearts and ambitions—usually to become his Queen and rule the kingdom in their own ways.

Not so this doctor, who had clearly never heard the word *submissive* in her life.

It was an adjustment, certainly.

"I had no idea you were being held here," Tarek told her. He lifted his mobile as if she could read the documents Ahmed had sent him while she ate. "But I have read your file."

"Would anything have been different if you had known?" she asked, and it wasn't precisely an interruption. He had paused.

Still. That, too, was different.

He reminded himself, with a touch of acid, that this was the woman who had cheerfully called him a pig while still behind bars. Unaware that he had come to liberate her, not punish her further.

Perhaps *blunt* and *forthright* did not quite cover it.

"I cannot alter the past, much as I would like to," he said. He studied her, and the easy way she held his gaze. As if she was the one measuring him, instead of the other way round. "Do you know why you were imprisoned in the first place?"

She let out a sharp little laugh of disbelief. Not a noise others generally made in his presence. "Do you?"

Again, he indicated his mobile. He did not react to the disrespectful tone. Much. "I know what was written in your file when you were taken into custody."

Another deeply impolite sound, not quite a laugh, that he congratulated himself on ignoring. "I believe the pretext for our arrest was an illegal border crossing. The fact that we were administering humanitarian aid and were in no way dissidents fomenting rebellion or revolution did not impress your police force. Mostly there was a lot of shouting. And guns."

"That was an upsetting period here," he agreed. "There was an attempt at a coup, as I mentioned. Dissidents tried to take the palace and there were a few, targeted uprisings around the country."

If he had only listened to his mother, he might have armored himself against the unforgivable affection that had allowed him to minimize his brother's behavior over the years. He'd convinced himself Rafiq's bad behavior was not a pattern. And even if it was, that it wasn't serious.

"*A man who will be King cannot allow love to make him a danger to his country*," his mother had warned him. "*What a man loves is his business. What a king loves can never be anything but a weapon used against him.*"

Tarek had never imagined that weapon would be a literal one. Or that he would wish, deeply and surpassingly, that he had listened more closely to his mother when he'd had the chance.

There was something about the sharp focus Anya trained on him, complete with a faint frown between her brows, that he liked a lot more than he should. When he knew he would consider it nothing short of an impertinence in anyone else. And would likely react badly.

But even this doctor's *focus* felt like passion to him.

"A coup? In the palace?" She waited for his nod. "You mean they came for you. Here."

"They did." He did not precisely smile. "More accurately, they tried."

Rafiq had tried. Personally. A bitter wound that Tarek doubted would ever truly heal.

Still, he had the strangest urge to show her his scars. An urge he repressed. But he found himself watching the way her expression changed, and telling himself there was a kind of respect there.

"You're lucky you have so many guards to protect you, then."

He opted not to analyze why that statement bothered him so much.

"I am," Tarek agreed, his voice cooler than it should have been, because it shouldn't have mattered to him what this woman thought—of him or the kingdom or anything else. "Though they were little help when my brother and his men tried to take me after what was meant to be a quiet family meal commemorating the two-month anniversary of our father's death."

He did not like the memory. He resented that he was forced to revisit it.

Yet Anya's expression didn't change and Tarek could feel her…paying closer attention, somehow. With the same ferocity she'd used while demolishing a plate of pastries earlier.

Why did that make him want her so desperately?

But even as he asked himself the question, he knew the answer. He could imagine, all too well, that fierce, intent focus of hers on his body. On what they could do together.

He wrestled himself under control and wasn't happy at how difficult it proved. "It was a confusing time. I regret that there were far more imprisonments than there should have been, and, indeed, your colleagues were released as soon as order was restored. But due to the vagaries of several archaic customs, you were not. I could explain why, but what matters is that the responsibility is mine."

She broke her intense scrutiny of him then, glancing away while her throat moved. "They were released? How long ago?"

"As I said, when order was restored to the kingdom."

She looked back at him, her eyes narrow. "Thank you. But is that a week ago? Seven months ago? Twenty-four hours after they were taken in?"

"I do not think they were incarcerated for very

long." That was no more and no less than the truth, as far as he knew it. He should not have felt that strange sense that he'd betrayed her, somehow. By telling her? Or by allowing it to happen in the first place—not that he'd known? Tarek felt the uncharacteristic shift about in his seat like a recalcitrant child. He restrained it. "No more than two months, I am given to understand."

Across from him, Anya sat very still in her gray, faded tunic, that hair of hers tumbling all around her. She shook her head, faintly, as if she was trying to shake off a cloud. Or perhaps confusion. "I was forgotten about?"

Tarek held her gaze, surprised to discover he did not want to. He reminded himself that this was the foremost duty of any king, like it or not. Accountability.

It didn't matter that he hadn't known she existed, much less that she and her colleagues had been caught up in the troubles here. Just as it didn't matter that he hadn't known until this very afternoon that she had been languishing in his very own dungeon. He was responsible all the same.

He might as well have slammed shut the iron door and turned the key himself.

Tarek inclined his head. "I'm afraid so."

She nodded, blinking a bit. Then she cleared her throat. "Thank you for your honesty."

And for a moment, there was quiet. She did not reach for more food from the platters before her.

She did not hold him in the intensity of her brown gaze, shot through with gold in the hectic light that filled this salon.

For a moment there was only the faint catch of her breath, hardly a sound at all. The sound of birds calling to each other outside. The lap of the fountain out on her terrace.

And the improbable beat of his own pulse, hard and heavy in his temples. His chest. His sex.

Tarek could not have said if it was longing…or shame.

He had so little experience with either.

"You should know that your presence here has created something of an international crisis," he said when he could take the pressing noise of the silence between them no longer. "Something else I'm embarrassed to say I was unaware of until today."

She smirked. "It's created a crisis for me, certainly. An unwanted and forced eight-month vacation from my life."

"I want to be clear about this," Tarek said. "Were you harmed in any way?"

"Define harm," she shot back. "I expected to be beaten. Abused."

"If this happened, you need only tell me and the perpetrators will be brought to justice. Harsh justice to suit their crimes. I swear this to you, here and now."

"None of those things happened," Anya said, but her voice was thicker than it had been before. "And maybe your plan is to throw me right back into that cell today, so let me assure you that it's an effective punishment. That cell is deceptively roomy, isn't it? It's still a cell, cut off from the world."

He leaned forward, searching her face. "But you were not harmed?"

Her lips pressed into a line. "How do you measure the harm of being captured, shouted at in a language you don't speak, separated from the rest of your colleagues, and then thrown into a cold stone cell? Then kept there for months, never knowing if today might be the day the real terror might begin? Or you might be trotted out for an execution? I don't know how to measure that. Do you?"

Tarek studied her closely. Looking for scars, perhaps. Or some hint of emotional fragility or tears, because that, he would understand. But instead, this woman looked at him as if she was also a warrior. As if she too had fought, in her own way.

He felt his own scars, hacked into his flesh in this very same palace, throbbing as if they were new.

"It is all unfortunate," he said quietly. "There are many ways to fight in a war, are there not? And so many of them are not what we would have chosen, had we been offered a choice."

"I'm a doctor," she replied, matching his tone. Her dark eyes tight on his. "When I go to war, it's to heal. Never to fight."

"We all fight, Doctor. With whatever tools we are

given. Whether you choose to admit that or do not is between you and whatever it is you pray to."

And for another long, impossibly fraught moment, they only stared at each other. Here where the desert sun made the walls shimmer and dance. A fitting antidote to the dungeon, he thought. Abundant, unavoidable sunshine made into a thousand different colors, until the sheer volume of it all made breath itself feel new.

But as the silence wore on, he found the glare she leveled on him with those sharp, clever eyes of hers far more intriguing.

Another thing he did not plan to look at too closely.

"Do you have more questions?" she asked. Eventually. "I find the longer I'm out of that cell, the harder it is not to want to scrub myself clean of the experience. Assuming, that is, that this isn't all a great ruse."

Tarek understood, then, how easy it would be if this was the trick she thought it was. His brother, for example, would have thought nothing of fabricating some explanation for keeping this woman locked up—a law she'd broken that no one could prove she hadn't—and then tossing her back down in the dungeon to rot. His treatment of his own staff had been the despair of the palace. Rafiq would not have cared about international opinion. If things grew tense, he would have closed the American embassy, shut the Alzalam borders, and continued to do as he pleased.

But Tarek was not his grasping, morally vacant younger brother. His vision of the kingdom did not involve petty tyrannies, no matter the inconvenience to him, personally.

"I am not the kind of man who plays games," he told her, which should have gone without saying. He accepted that she was unlikely to know this about him. "Ruses of any kind do not impress me nor appeal to me. You will not be returning to that cell, or any other cell in my kingdom."

"Because you say so?"

"Because I am the King and so decree it."

"That sounds impressive." She did not sound impressed.

He shoved that aside. "But should you choose to reach out to the outside world, I would have you recognize that the moment I knew of your imprisonment, you were released."

She blinked again. Tarek wondered if he was watching her *think*. And sure enough, her gaze sharpened even further in the next moment. "Wait. My imprisonment is your crisis? Not my *presence*. But the actual fact that I've been locked away for eight months."

There were so many things he could have said to that. He entertained them all, then dismissed them, one by one.

"Yes."

Anya's lips quirked. "What level of crisis are we talking about here?"

"I have not had time to study it in any detail, I am afraid. As I was more focused on removing you from the dungeon as quickly as possible."

"Your mercy knows no bounds, I'm sure."

These were extraordinary circumstances and she was the victim in this, so Tarek ignored the insolent tone. Though it caused him physical pain to do so.

Or perhaps you only wish for an excuse to touch her, something insidious and too warm within him whispered.

"My understanding is that your imprisonment is considered a humanitarian crisis in many Western countries. And as our papers have only recently begun discussing the outside world again, after this long year of unrest, it has gone on far longer than it should have."

Anya nodded. "And I'm not a thoughtless tourist smuggling in drugs in a stranger's teddy bear, am I? That can't look good for you."

Tarek unclenched his jaw. "As a token of my embarrassment and a gesture of goodwill, I will throw a dinner this very night. We will invite your ambassador. You can assure him, in your own words, that you are safe and well."

That little smirk of hers deepened. "And what if I'm neither safe nor well?"

Tarek wanted to argue. She had eaten, she was sparring with him—*him*—and a glance at her cell had told him that she had not been suffering unduly while in custody. There were far greater ills. As a doctor, she should know that.

But he thought better of saying such things. What did he know about Americans? Perhaps the harm she'd spoken of was real enough. She could not possibly have been raised as hardy as the local women. Equal to sandstorms and blazing heat alike, all while keeping themselves looking soft and yielding.

It was only kind to make allowances for her upbringing.

"Then you may tell the ambassador of your suffering," he said instead of what he wanted to say. Magnanimously, he thought. "You may tell him whatever you wish."

"You will have to forgive me," Anya said, sounding almost careful. It was a marked contrast to how she'd spoken to him before, with such familiarity. "But I can't quite wrap my head around this. I expect to be seized again at any moment and dragged back to the dungeon. I certainly can't quite believe that the King of Alzalam is perfectly happy to give me carte blanche to tell any story I like to an ambassador. Or to anyone else."

Tarek made his decision then and there. The plan that was forming in his head was outrageous. Absurd on too many levels to count. But the more it settled in him, the more he liked it.

It was simple, really. Elegant.

And while bracing honesty was not something he had ever imagined would factor into his usual relationships with women, such as his betrothal, this woman was different. If she wasn't, she would not have ended up in his dungeon. She would certainly not have been here, telling him to his face that she doubted what he said to her. His word, which was law.

He ought to have been outraged. Instead, he accepted that he had to treat his doctor…differently.

It wouldn't be the first time in this long and difficult year that he'd had to change strategy on the fly. To set aside old plans and come up with new ones, then implement them immediately. Tarek liked to think he'd developed a talent for it.

The kingdom was ancient. Yet the King could not be similarly made of stone, or he would be the first to crumble. His father had taught him that, his mother had tried to warn him, but Tarek had lived it.

"Of course I wish that I could control what it is you might say about your time here," he told her, and watched the shock of that hit her, making her fall back in her seat. "I have no wish to be thought a monster, and I would love nothing more than to present your emancipation…carefully and in a way that brings, if not honor to the kingdom, no greater shame. But that is not up to me."

If Tarek was not mistaken, that dazed light in her eyes meant he had succeeded in being…disarming. Imagine that.

He continued in the same vein. "I will leave it up to you. You have no reason to trust me, so I will not ask such a thing of you. I would request only this. That if asked, you make it known that the very moment I learned that you were here, I freed you myself."

That dazed light faded, replaced by something far sharper.

"You want me to be your press release," she said softly.

"I would love you to be my press release." He even laughed, and as he did, it occurred to him that he wasn't faking this. "If there exists any possibility that you will sing wide the glory of the kingdom, I would be delighted."

Her head tilted slightly to one side, and Tarek still wasn't used to her direct gaze. To the way she unapologetically *considered* him, right where he could see her do it. "I can't speak to any possibilities or press releases, I'm afraid. I haven't taken a proper shower in eight months. Much less soaked myself in a good, long bath. Or used moisturizer. Or any of a thousand other everyday things that now seem luxurious to me."

"I understand, of course." Tarek smiled, again astonished to discover it was not a forced smile. He did not think of honey or vinegar, bees or business. Only what he could do to make her look at him without suspicion. "You must do what you feel is right."

He should not have taken pleasure in the way she looked at him, as if he wasn't quite what she expected. Surely he should not have introduced *pleasure* into this in the first place, no matter how tempting she was when she ate so recklessly, so heedlessly.

Tarek could not help but wonder how else she might approach her appetites. How else she might choose to sate them.

That is enough for now, he snapped at himself.

He stood, inclining his head to her in what he doubted she would realize was more of an apology than anything he might have said. Or would say.

"I will leave you to your luxuries, Doctor," he said. He nodded toward the door. "As I mentioned before, my staff waits outside to attend to you, should you wish it. This suite has both indoor and outdoor spaces, so you need not feel confined. Should you have need of me, personally, I will make myself available to you. You need only ask."

Her eyes darted around the room as if she was looking for a way out. Or for a lie. "Um. Yes. Thank you."

And Tarek left her then, aware as he strode from the room that he was battling the most unusual sensation.

Not fury at the circumstances.

Not distaste at what fate had thrown before him on this day, just as he'd imagined he was over the worst of this complicated year and ready to settle into a brighter future.

Not the usual bitterness that surged in him when he thought of his brother's betrayal.

But the exceptionally unusual feeling that, even though all she was doing was fencing words with him—with an insolence Tarek would have permitted from no other—he would have preferred to stay.

CHAPTER FOUR

THE BATHROOM ALONE was at least three times the size of her cell, and Anya intended to enjoy every inch of it.

She spent a long while in the vast shower, with its numerous jets and showerheads, offering her every possible water experience imaginable. She conditioned her hair three separate times. She slathered herself in all the shower creams and gels and soaps available. When she was done, having scrubbed every inch of her body to get the dungeon off, she drew a bath in a freestanding tub. She filled it with salts that felt like silk against her skin and she sat in the water for a long while, letting emotion work itself through her in waves. She stared out the windows, sank down deeper into the embrace of the water, and let whatever was inside her work its way through her while she breathed.

And pretended it was the steam on her cheeks, nothing more.

After her bath, she wrapped herself in one of the

exultantly thick robes that hung on the wall, and sat at the vanity piled high with every hair implement she'd ever dreamed of. And a great many more she'd never seen before. Then she thought of absolutely nothing while she blew out her hair, then put in a few well-placed curls, until the woman who looked back at her from the mirror was actually…her again.

"Me," she whispered out loud.

Her chest felt so tight it hurt to breathe, but she made herself do it anyway—long and deep—trying to keep that knotted thing below her breastbone at bay.

Anya got up then, snuggling deeper into the lush embrace of the robe. Now that she was so clean she was pickled, she let herself explore. She enjoyed her bare feet against the cool stone floors, or sunk deep into the thick rugs. She wandered the halls, going in and out of each of the bright rooms, then out onto the wide terrace so she could stand beneath the sky.

She hadn't invited any staff inside, because that felt too much like more guards. Instead, she wandered around all on her own, as thrilled with the fact she was alone as anything else. All alone. No one was watching her. No one was listening to her. It amazed her how much she'd missed the simple freedom of walking through a room unobserved.

Through all the rooms. A media center with screens of all descriptions. There was that brightly colored room she'd sat in with Tarek, and three other salons, one for every mood or hint of weather. She had her own little courtyard, filled with flowers, plants, and a fountain that spilled into a pretty pool. There was a fully outfitted gym, two different office spaces, each with a different view, and a small library.

There was also a selection of bedchambers. Anya went into each, testing the softness of the mattresses and sitting in the chairs or lounging on the chaises, because she could. And because it made her feel like Goldilocks. But she knew the moment she entered the master suite. There was the foyer of mosaic. The art on the walls.

In the bedchamber itself, she found a glorious, four-poster bed that could sleep ten, which made her feel emotional all over again.

And laid out on top of the brightly colored bed linens, a rugged-looking canvas bag that she stared at as if it was a ghost.

Because it was. The last time Anya had seen it, the police had taken it from her.

Suddenly trembling, she moved to the end of the bed, staring at her bag as if she thought it might… explode. Or she might. And then, making strange noises as if her body couldn't decide if she was breathing or sobbing, she pulled her bag toward her. Beneath it she found the jeans, T-shirt, and overtunic she'd been wearing that night. The scarf she'd had wrapped around her head. And inside the bag, her personal medical kit, her passport, and her mobile.

Charged, she saw when she switched it on. Anya

stayed frozen where she was, staring at the phone in her hand and the now unfamiliar weight of it. Her voice mailbox was full. There were thousands of emails waiting. Notifications from apps she'd all but forgotten about.

The outside world in a tiny little box in her palm. And after all this time—all the days and nights she'd made long and complicated lists of all the people she would contact first, all the calls she would make, all the messages she would send—what she did was drop the mobile back down onto the bed.

And then back away as if it was a snake.

Her heart began to race. Nausea bloomed, then worked its way through her. Her breath picked up, and then the panic slammed straight into her.

It didn't matter what she told herself. It never had mattered. Anya sank down onto her knees and then, when that wasn't sufficiently low enough, collapsed onto her belly. And as it had so many times before, the panic took control.

"You are not dying," she chanted at herself. "It only feels like it."

Her heart pounded so hard, so loud, it seemed impossible to her that she wasn't having a major cardiac event. She ordered herself to stop hyperventilating, because the doctor in her knew that made it worse, but that didn't work. It never worked.

Anya cried then, soundless, shaking sobs. Because it felt like she was dying, and she couldn't bear it—not when she'd only just escaped that dungeon.

But she knew that there was no fighting these panic attacks when they came. That was the horror of them. There was only surrendering, and she had never been any good at that.

It felt like an eternity. Eventually, she managed to breathe better, slowing each breath and using her nose more than her mouth. Slowly, her heart beat less frantically.

Slowly, slowly, the clench of nausea dissipated.

But she still had to crawl across the floor on her hands and knees. Back into the bathroom, where she had to lie for a while on the cold marble floor. Just to make sure that *this time* it really wasn't the sudden onset of a horrible influenza.

As she lay there, staring balefully at the literally palatial toilet before her, it occurred to her that in all the months she'd been imprisoned, she'd never once had one of these attacks. If asked, Anya would have said that her whole life had taken place on a level of intense stress and fear. Especially before she'd begun to learn the language, and had been forced to exist in a swirl of uncomprehending terror.

Stress, fear, and terror, sure. But she hadn't had one of these vicious little panic attacks, had she?

And in fact, it was only when she thought about the world contained on her mobile—and the inevitable messages she would find from her father—that her heart kicked at her again. And another queasy jolt hit her straight in the belly. She could feel her shoulders seem to tie themselves into dramatic shapes above her head, and apparently, it was here on the bathroom floor of a grand palace in Alzalam that Anya might just have to face the fact that it wasn't her eight-month imprisonment that really stressed her out.

It was the life she'd put on hold while stuck in that cell.

"That's ridiculous," she muttered at herself as she pulled herself up and onto her feet, feeling brittle and significantly older than she had before.

When she staggered back out of the bathroom, she didn't head for her bag again. Or her mobile, God forbid. She went instead through the far archway and found herself in an expansive dressing room, stocked full of clothing, just as the forbidding and beautiful Tarek had promised.

Anya told herself that she was erring on the side of caution. But she suspected it was more that she didn't want to be alone any longer, stuck with nothing but her panic, too many voice mail messages she didn't want to listen to, and the horror of her inbox.

Whatever it was, she went out and called in the servants.

"I am to have dinner with the Sheikh and the American ambassador," she told the two women who waited for her, both of them smiling as if they'd waited their entire lives for this opportunity.

"Yes, madam," one of them said. "Such an honor."

Anya had not considered it an honor. Should she have? When Tarek had made it clear that it was likely damage control? Maybe she really did need to sit down with her mobile, get online, and read the story of what had happened to her as told by people she'd never met. But the thought of picking up that phone again made something cold roll down her spine.

She smiled back at the women. "I'm hoping you can help me. I've never attended a formal dinner in your country and I have been…indisposed for so long."

"Don't you worry, madam," said the other woman, smiling even brighter. "We will make you shine."

And that was what they did.

They spared no detail. They buffed Anya's fingernails and her toenails, then added polish. They clucked disapprovingly over her brows, and then, as far she could tell, removed every errant piece of hair from her entire body. There was a salt scrub, because they did not feel that her long shower, or deep soak in the bath, was up to par.

Nor were they impressed with her hair, and when they were finished restyling it, she could see why. Anya looked luminous. Soft, pampered, and something like happy.

They had rimmed her eyes with dark mascara. They'd slicked a soft gloss over her lips. And when she looked in the set of full-length mirrors in the dressing room, she found herself resplendent in a bright tunic and matching trousers, flowing and lovely. Topped off with a long scarf with a pretty, jeweled edge that complemented the outfit and made her seem like someone else. The kind of woman who dined with ambassadors and kings, maybe.

"Thank you," she said to the women when they were done. "You've worked miracles here tonight."

Anya found herself smiling when they led her out of her rooms, then through the halls of the palace.

Night was falling outside, but the palace was still filled with light. She could see the last of the sun creep away a bit more every time they walked across a courtyard. And when they reached the grand central courtyard—that she vaguely remembered studying on the plane out of Houston a lifetime ago, because she'd known she was heading into the region—she paused for a moment as the night took over the sky.

Because she wasn't in the cell. There was nothing between her and the stars, save the palace walls that stood, then, at a distance. As if they understood, the women seemed content to wait while she stood there, her head tipped back and the half-wild notion that if she jumped, she would float straight off into the galaxy.

But she didn't. And when she came back to earth, the servants led her into a smaller room off the courtyard that was filled with Americans.

"His Excellency wishes you to speak with your countrymen for long as you desire," the woman closest to her said, not in English. "Only when you are satisfied will the formal dinner begin."

"Thank you," Anya said quietly.

"You learned the language?" asked one of the men who waited for her, slick and polished in his suit and shiny shoes, with a sharp smile to match. "Smart move, Dr. Turner."

Anya heard the door close behind her, and surely she should have felt…something different, now. Some sense of triumph, or victory. Instead, she felt almost as if she was back in one of the hospitals she'd worked in before she'd come abroad, forced to contend with competitive doctors and high-stakes medical issues alike.

There were too many men in suits in the room and somehow, what she wanted was a different man. One in ivory and gold, with a predator's sharp gaze, and the quiet, inarguable presence of heavy stone.

"Was it smart?" she asked, smiling faintly because she thought she should. "Or survival?"

"It's an honor to meet you, Dr. Turner," said the most polished of the men, his face creased with wisdom and his smile encouraging. "I'm Ambassador Pomeroy, and I have to tell you, I can't wait to take you home."

Home. That word echoed around inside of her. And as the circle of men tightened around her, all of them making soothing noises and asking about her state of mind and general welfare, she told herself it was joy.

Because it had to be joy.

But it wasn't until she walked into the dining room that had been prepared for them—another triumph of mosaic and marble, beautifully lit and welcoming—that she breathed easy again.

Because Tarek waited there, lounging with seeming carelessness at the head of a long table. His gaze was hooded and dark, a clear indication of the power he was choosing not to wield, so obvious to Anya that it made her feel hollowed out with a kind of shiver. He was wearing a different set of robes that should have made him look silly compared to the pack of American diplomats in their business suits. But didn't.

At all.

"Welcome," the King said, his voice a ruthless scrape across the pretty room. "I thank you for joining me in this celebration of—" and Anya could have sworn that he looked only at her, then "—resilience and grace."

"Hear, hear," cried the men, a bit too brightly for strangers.

And despite how she'd feasted earlier, and how sure she'd been that she couldn't eat another bite, she found when she was seated at Tarek's right hand that she was starving. So while the men engaged in the sort of elegantly poisonous dinner conversation that she supposed was the hallmark of international diplomacy, or perhaps of tedious dinner parties, Anya indulged herself. Again.

It was only when she was quietly marveling at the tenderness of the chicken she was eating—simmered to tear-jerking tenderness on a bed of fragrant rice and doused in a thick, spicy sauce with so many *flavors*—that Anya realized that the Sheikh was not paying any attention to the arch wordplay of the ambassador and his aides.

Instead, Tarek was focused on her.

"The food in the dungeon wasn't terrible," she told him, realizing only as she smiled at him that she was... not embarrassed, exactly. But something in her heated up and stayed hot at the notion he was watching her again. "Just, you know. Bland."

"That is unpardonable."

Was she imagining the heat in his gaze? The faint trace of humor in that dark voice of his?

"How did you find your ambassador?" he asked, doing something with his chin that brought one of the waiting servants over to place more delicacies in front of her. "Appropriately outraged on your behalf, I trust?"

"Are you asking if I issued that press release?" she heard herself ask, in a tone she was terribly afraid was more flirtatious than not.

Good lord. Maybe when she'd had that panic attack, she'd hit her head on the stone floor. That was the only explanation. She dropped her gaze to her plate.

But she could still feel Tarek beside her. The burn of his attention all over her.

"I have a far more interesting question to ask you than what you did or did not tell a career diplomat," he said, all quiet force and the dark beneath. Like the night sky she'd wanted to float away in, ripe with stars. "Who will tell his own tales to suit himself, let me assure you."

Anya's heart was picking up speed again, but this time, without all the other telltale signs that she was descending into a panic attack. Because she wasn't.

She recognized the heat. And what felt an awful lot like need, curling inside her, like flame.

It had been there from the moment she'd first seen him. And now, buffed and plucked and polished to please, she understood that it had been for him as much as for her. She'd felt pretty in her mirror.

But when Tarek looked at her, she felt alive.

It was crazy. Maybe *she* was crazy. At the very least, she needed to leave this country and sort out what had happened to her—and how she felt about it—far, far away from the very dungeon where she'd been held all this time. This was likely nothing more than PTSD.

But tell that to the softest part of her, that melted as she sat there.

"You appear to be filled with questions," she said. Less flirtatiously, to her credit.

"I have spent a long year as a man of action, primarily," he said, and she made a note to look up the coup he'd mentioned. And what he'd done to combat it when his brother had been involved. "But I have always found that intellectual rigor is the true measure of a person. For without it, what separates us from the beasts?"

Anya forgot the plates piled high before her. "Some would say a soul."

"What would you say?"

She was dimly aware that they were not alone. That the ambassador and his aides were still at the same table, sharing the same meal. But she couldn't have said where they were seated. Or what they were talking about. Or even what any of them looked like.

It was as if there was only Tarek.

"I think that when everything is taken from you, what's left is the soul," she said quietly. "And it is up to you if that sustains you or scares you, I suppose."

There was a different, considering light in his gaze then. "What did you find, then?"

Something in her trembled, though she knew it wasn't fear. But it was as if some kind of foreboding kept her from answering him, all the same. Instead, she made herself smile to break the sudden tension between them. She reminded herself that they were not alone in this room, no matter how it felt.

And that he might have told her that he intended to be honest, but that didn't make it true. He was a very powerful, very canny king who had proved that he was more than capable of holding on to his throne, the ambassador had told her earlier.

"*He is not to be underestimated,*" the man had said.

Anya spread open her hands, shrugging. "Here I am. I suppose that means that I found a way to sustain myself, whatever it took."

Tarek lifted the glass before him, sitting back in his chair. He looked every inch the monarch. Currently indulgent, but with that severity lurking beneath.

She should certainly not have found him remotely compelling.

She told herself that of course she didn't.

Yet as the dinner wore on, she admitted privately that something about this man seemed to be lodged beneath her skin. She might have told herself it was simply because he was the first truly, inarguably beautiful man she'd seen since her ordeal had begun. But a glance around the table put paid to that idea.

Because the ambassador's men were all perfectly attractive. She could see that…but she didn't *feel* it. Her body didn't care at all about these bland men with their overly wide smiles and targeted geniality.

But the brooding, dangerous Sheikh who could have them all executed with one of those tiny flicks of his finger made her pulse pound.

Anya made a mental note to seek out psychiatric help the moment she returned to American soil.

"We're prepared to take you to the embassy tonight," the ambassador said at the end of the meal. "You must be anxious to leave the palace behind."

His smile was slick and aimed directly at Tarek.

Tarek looked faintly bored, as if these discussions were beneath him. "Dr. Turner is, of course, welcome to do as she pleases."

Anya thought that what would have pleased Dr. Turner the most would have been to remain full and happy again, without the unmistakable tension that filled the room. Especially because she doubted very much that any of the diplomats particularly cared about her feelings in this. She was a figure. A cause.

She was tired of being something other than a woman.

"I thought I made this clear before dinner," she said, as if she was concerned that the ambassador had gotten the wrong end of the stick when she knew very well he hadn't. "I'm not being *held* here. Not anymore."

Though it took everything she had in her not to look at Tarek when she said that, to see if that was actually true.

"I know it suits you to think of me as your pet barbarian," Tarek said to the ambassador, in a voice of silk and peril. "But I am nothing so interesting as a monster, I am afraid. Some things are regrettable mistakes, nothing more."

"Then there should be no trouble removing Dr. Turner from your custody," Ambassador Pomeroy replied with a toothy smile. "The American people would breathe a little easier, knowing she was safe at last."

"That is entirely up to Dr. Turner," Tarek replied. "As I have said."

Anya thought of her mobile, still on her bed back in her suite. She thought of the life that waited for her, in that phone and back in the States. Of the time she'd spent in Houston. Of her father.

Mostly she thought of Tarek, the heat in his dark gaze, and the question he had yet to ask her.

Because she knew he hadn't forgotten. Neither had she.

She picked up the linen napkin in her lap and dabbed gently at the corner of her mouth. "I would love to put the American people at ease. And I appreciate your assistance, Ambassador." She smiled, as punctuation. Or performance, maybe. It was hard to tell with so much molten heat making her ache. "But I spent eight months locked beneath this palace. I'm going to spend at least one night sleeping like a princess before I go. It's literally the very least this palace can do for me."

There were protestations. Some dire mutterings from the ambassador and far louder commentary from his aides. Still, eventually, they left her to the fate she was almost certain she already regretted choosing.

Yet Anya didn't open up her mouth and change that fate, even though she knew she could. And almost certainly should.

When the palace staff retreated after the Americans had left, she found herself once again alone in a room with this obviously ruthless man who really should not have fascinated her the way he did.

Especially when he took a long, simmering sort of look at her, setting fire to the quiet between them.

"I take it your rooms are to your liking, then," Tarek said, almost idly. "And though I am glad of it, surely you must be in a great hurry to resume your life. To see your family, your friends. To pick up where you left off eight months ago."

Anya felt that knot in her chest tighten a painful inch or two. "The funny thing about spending so long locked away is how little some things seem to matter, in the end. My friends are scattered all over the globe. I miss them, but we're used to not seeing each other. And my life had become nomadic. I haven't truly *lived* in a place since I left my last hospital job in Houston."

He was watching her almost too closely. "And your family?"

"It's only my father and his wife." She could feel herself getting tighter, everywhere, and was horrified at the idea she might collapse into panic here. With him. "We aren't close."

Anya didn't want to talk to him about accommodations or her lonely little life. Not now they were alone. Not now he seemed looser as he sat there. Lazier, almost, though she did not for one second mistake that leashed power in him for anything else. She could feel it as if it was a third presence in the room.

She could feel it inside her, turning her to flame.

Anya frowned at him. "Is that the question you wanted to ask me?"

He laughed at that, as if it was funny, when she felt so sure that it was crucial that he ask her his question. That it was *fate*.

But he was laughing. And Anya took the opportunity to ask herself what she was doing here. Why wasn't she on her way to the American embassy right now? And if she really wanted to sleep in that glorious bed—which she truly did, after a prison cot— why wasn't she up in that suite right now, continuing to pamper herself?

Why was she sitting here next to Tarek, imprisoning herself by choice, as if he was cupping her between his palms?

Worse still, she had the distinct sensation that he knew it.

"It is more a proposition than a question," he told her.

And Anya did not need to let that word kick around inside her, leaving trails of dangerous sparks behind. But she didn't do a thing to stop it. "Do you often proposition your former captives?"

"Not quite like this, Doctor." He didn't smile then, though she thought his eyes gleamed. And she felt the molten heat of it, the wild flame. She thought she saw stars again, but it was only Tarek, gazing back at her. "I want you to marry me."

CHAPTER FIVE

"*MARRY* YOU?" HIS suspicious doctor echoed.

Notably not in tones of awe and gratitude, which Tarek would have expected as his due from any other woman not currently seeking asylum in the Canadian provinces.

But then, that somehow felt to Tarek like confirmation that this woman was the correct choice for this complicated moment in Alzalam's history. And for him, because she was…different. A challenge, when women had always been an afterthought at best for him.

"It is an easy solution to a thorny problem." He watched, fascinated, as a hint of color asserted itself on her fine cheeks. "I assume you acquainted yourself with the media coverage of your case before dinner."

Her color deepened. "I did not."

He lifted his brows. "Did you not? I find that surprising."

She moved her shoulders, but it was less a straightening, or even a shrug. It was more…discomfort, he thought. And he found he liked the idea that she was not immune to him, to this. That he was not the only one wrestling with entirely too much sensation.

"I haven't had access to the internet for a long time," she said after a moment. "It seemed almost too much, really. I'm sure that will pass and I'll find myself addicted to scrolling aimlessly again. Isn't everyone?"

Tarek did not allow himself the weakness of addiction. But he did not say this here, now. He liked, perhaps too much, that she had not raced off to look herself up. That the stories others told about her—and about him—had not been her first priority.

That she was in no hurry to resume her old life could only support his proposition, surely.

He should not have let that notion work in him like heat. "I assume your ambassador and his men shared with you that you have become something of a cause célèbre."

Anya didn't meet his gaze. And though he hadn't known her long at all, it was clear that looking away was not usual for this woman. She was all about her directness. She was forthright and pointed. A scalpel, not a soft veil.

That, too, was its own heat inside him.

"I don't exactly know how to process the notion that anyone knows who I am," she said after a moment. "I know some people enjoy being talked about like that, but I'm not one of them."

"Allow me to recap," Tarek offered, sitting back in

his chair so he would not indulge himself and touch her. Though he marveled at how much he wished to do so. "Because I did spend the evening catching up on the sad tale of the American doctor we so cruelly imprisoned here while handling a small, inconsequential revolution. After she illegally crossed our border."

Her gaze snapped to his then, and Tarek wondered why it was he preferred her temper when he would not have tolerated it from anyone else.

"Careful," she said softly. "The mocking tone doesn't help your case."

"Forgive me. It is only that looking at you, it is hard to imagine that you suffered at all." She looked too ripe. She glowed. She was… *You must remain calm*, he ordered himself, when he could not recall the last time he was not calm. Supernaturally calm, his brother had once claimed. It was only now that Tarek understood that had been a warning he should have heeded. "I know, of course, that is not the case."

"You're always welcome to lock yourself away for eight months and see how you enjoy the experience." Her smile was sharp. "I wonder how you'd look at the end of it."

He felt his lips curve despite himself. "Touché. Consider me adequately chastened."

Her smiled lost its sharpness. "You were telling me my story."

"Indeed. The fact is, while there was certainly interest in all the doctors disappearing that night, when the male doctors were returned but you were not, it created…consternation."

She looked amused. "Consternation?"

"Concern," he amended. "The news reports have been increasingly more frantic as time has gone on."

"I'm surprised the ambassador didn't insist upon seeing me sooner, then." Her gaze darkened. "Or at all."

"There is no possibility that the ambassador could have visited you before now," Tarek assured her, not pleased with that sudden darkness. Not pleased at all. "At the best of times, the palace does not comment on internal matters and therefore, never confirmed nor denied that you were held here. And during the troubles, the palace was locked down completely. There was no access. Regrettably, what that meant was that as far as the world knew, you went into the same prison as your colleagues, then disappeared."

She toyed with the gleaming edge of her scarf. "That does sound dramatic."

"Had I been less preoccupied with putting down a coup and suffering through the very public trial of my own brother for high treason, I would have paid more attention to international headlines myself."

"I am moved, truly, by this non-apology."

Again, he found himself moved to smile when surely he should rage. "Alas, my focus was on putting my kingdom back together. That brings us to today and your immediate release once I learned of your incarceration."

"And your solution to this tale of the world's cruel mischaracterization of your perseverance is…marriage?" Anya laughed, and even though Tarek knew the laugh was directed at him, he found himself…entertained. Or not furious, anyway, which amounted to the same thing. "Maybe you can explain to me why the King of Alzalam, who surely could marry anyone, would want to marry a woman he quite literally lifted out of a cell."

"It is practical," he told her, though the heat in him was surely nothing of the kind. "You could not have suffered any great abuses here, could you, if you end up marrying me. Your experience will be seen as romantic."

"A romantic imprisonment." Her tone was dubious. "I don't think that's a thing."

Tarek only smiled. "Is it not?"

She flushed again, and he felt that too distinctly. Like her hands on him.

He took pity on her. "Western audiences live for romantic love. They insert it into the most unlikely scenarios. You must know this is so. How many stalkers do you suppose are heralded as romantic heroes? I can think of dozens and I am no particular aficionado of your Western stories, no matter the media."

"I think you underestimate the difference between fiction and reality," she replied, no longer looking or sounding the least bit flustered. "And hard as it might be for you to imagine, the average Western woman is perfectly capable of judging the difference between the two."

"But is the average Western journalist capable of the same?" Tarek shrugged. "I do not think so."

Anya nodded slowly, as if taking it all on board. "This is all a bit out of left field, but I understand where you're coming from. It even makes a kind of sense. But what can you imagine is in it for me?"

The answer should have been self-evident, but Tarek could not allow himself to dwell on the day's indignities. "That is where it comes in handy that I am the King."

"I see that more as a detracting factor, to be honest, given my people gave up on kings in the seventeen hundreds."

"Ah, yes, the lure of independence. So attractive." He waved a hand. "But this is not practical, Anya. You can find independence anywhere. Meanwhile, I am a very powerful, very wealthy man. A sheikh and a king who can, if I desire, make my wishes into law. Tell me what you want and I will make it so. Anything at all."

"For all you know I'm going to ask for a spaceship."

"Then one shall be built for you." He bit back his smile. "Is that what you want? I assumed it would be more along the lines of wishing to practice medicine here in the capital city, even once you become Queen."

But to his surprise, she paled at that.

He didn't know quite how to feel about it when she

blew out a breath, then met his gaze once more as if she hadn't had that extreme reaction. "You say that as if a female doctor is as fantastical as a spaceship."

But Tarek found he liked her spiky voice better than watching her pale before him.

"Alzalam is not in the Stone Age, Doctor," he murmured. "No matter what foreign publications may imagine. We have a great many female doctors. But what we do not have, and never have had, are queens who work. Perhaps that is an oversight."

Anya huffed out another breath, as if she couldn't comprehend that. "I have to tell you, of all the endings I imagined to my time in prison, talk of queens did not enter into it."

She was too pretty, he thought. And getting more so by the moment, to his mind. Because he liked her bold. He liked how little she seemed in awe of him. He could not deny that he also liked the hint of vulnerability he saw now.

Did he want to give her a throne or did he simply want to take her to bed?

Tarek found he couldn't answer the question. Normally, that would have been all the convincing he needed that he was headed down the wrong path. He had never let a woman turn his head and he would have sworn on Alzalam itself that he never would.

But then, when it came to his doctor, there were practical considerations that outweighed everything else. Trade implications, for example, and potential sanctions. He could weather those, as his ancestors had upon occasion, but if there was no need to put himself in bed with only those economies who did not fear the taint of a regime considered monstrous, why would he condemn his country to such a struggle?

That he found himself longing to taste her was a problem when his country was at stake. Tarek tried to focus. "You have yet to tell me what it is you want most, Anya."

Had he said her name aloud before? He couldn't recall it. But it sizzled there, on his tongue. It felt far more intimate than it should. And in case he was tempted to imagine that it was only he who felt these things, he saw her eyes widen—her pupils dilating— as she sat there within reach.

But he did not use his hands. Not yet.

"I'm going to tell you something I've never told anyone before," Anya said, her voice softer than he had ever heard it. She leaned forward, the flowing scarf she wore making even the way she breathed look like a dance. She propped her elbows on the table and smiled at him over the top of the fingers she linked together. "I don't know why. Maybe it's because you're a stranger. A stranger who asked me to marry him after locking me up. If I can't tell you my secrets, who can I tell?"

"Tell me your secrets, Anya," he found himself saying, when he shouldn't. When he ought to have known better. "And I will show you my scars."

He was fascinated by watching her *think*. He

watched her blink, then her head tilted slightly to one side as her gaze moved all over him. "Are your scars secret?"

"Naturally." Tarek kept his tone careless when he felt anything but. "Who wishes to see that their King is little more than a mortal man, frail and easily wounded?"

It seemed to take her longer than usual to swallow. "But surely the point of a king is that he is a man first."

"A king is only a man when he fails," Tarek bit out. He gazed at her until he saw, once more, that telltale heat stain her cheeks. "But first you must tell me your secrets. That is the bargain."

"My father is a doctor," she said, and he had the notion the words tumbled from her, as if she'd loosed a dam of some kind and could no more control them than if they'd been a rush of water. "Not only a doctor, mind you. He's one of the foremost neurosurgeons in the country. Possibly the world. He would tell you that he is *the* foremost neurosurgeon, full stop. Even now, years past what others consider their prime, his hands are like steel. He's deeply proud of that."

"Is this secret you plan to tell me actually his secret? I will confess I find myself less interested in the deep, dark secrets of a man I have never met."

Anya sighed. "Surgeons are a very particular type of doctor. A very particular type of person, really. They don't think that they're God. They know it."

"My father was a king, Anya. I am familiar with the type."

Her smile flashed, an unexpected gift. "And look at you, not only happy to be your father's heir but apparently prepared to fight off a revolution so you can assume your throne after him, as planned."

It was tempting to thunder at her about duty and blood, but Tarek did not. He thought instead of what it was she was implying with her words. None of it having to do with him.

He chose to simply sit and watch her. To wait.

"There was never any question that I would become a doctor as well," Anya said, her voice something like careful. "To be honest, I don't know if I would have been permitted to imagine a different path for myself. My mother died when I was small and I wish I could remember what my father was like with her, but I don't. After she was gone I had a succession of stepmothers, each younger and more beautiful than the last. My father liked to praise their beauty while making a point of letting me know that the only thing he was interested in from me was my intellect. It never occurred to me to rebel. Or even to question. It was what he wanted that mattered. But then, for a long time, I wanted it as well. I wanted to show him that I could be smart like him, not merely a pretty plaything, easily ignored, like the stepmothers he replaced so easily. I wanted to make certain I was *special*."

Tarek waited still, his gaze on her and the storm in her eyes.

"But when it came time to pick my specialty in medical school," she said quietly, "I failed him."

"I do not understand." Tarek lifted a brow. "You are a doctor, are you not?"

"My father likes to refer to emergency medicine as fast food," Anya said. She shook her head. "Where's the art? Where's the glory? It's all triage, addicts, and Band-Aids slapped over broken limbs while bureaucrats count beds. That's a quote."

"But you knew his opinion and you did it anyway."

Anya smiled again, though it was a sad curve that didn't quite reach her eyes. "That was my form of rebellion. My father accused me of being afraid of the responsibility a surgeon must assume. He's not wrong."

Tarek was baffled. "Surely handling emergencies requires you to save lives. Potentially more lives than a brain surgeon, if we are to count volume alone."

"Sometimes he would sneer that it was ego. Mine. That I was afraid to enter into the same arena as him because he was so clearly superior to me. And that might have had something to do with my choices, I can't deny it. But mostly, I didn't want to compete with him." She took a breath. "It took a long while for me to recognize that it wasn't that I didn't want to be a surgeon. It's that really, I never wanted to be a doctor."

Tarek noticed her fingers were trembling, as if she'd just confessed to treason. He supposed, by her metric, she had.

"I couldn't tell him this," she continued, her voice shaking along with her fingers. "I couldn't tell anybody this. After all those years of study. All that work. All that knowledge stuck in my head forever. People are *called* to be doctors—isn't that what everyone wants to believe? You're supposed to want to help others, always. Even if it means sacrificing yourself." She paused to take another shaky breath. "My father is unpleasant in a great many ways, but day in and day out, he saves lives no one else can. How could I tell him that having already failed to live up to his example, I was actually, deep down, not even a shell of a decent person because I didn't want to anymore?"

Tarek waited, but he no longer felt the least bit lazy. Or even indulgent. He was coiled too tight, because he could see the turmoil in Anya's gaze. All over her face. And she was gripping her hands together, so tight that he could see her knuckles turn white.

"I couldn't tell him any of that," she said, answering herself. "I simply quit. I walked out of my job and refused to go back. I signed up for the charity the next day, ensuring that I couldn't have gone back even if I'd wanted to. And I don't know why I didn't tell him everything then, because believe me, Dr.

Preston Turner was not on board with me heading off to what he called *sleep-away camp for doctors*."

"I am fascinated by this man," Tarek drawled, sounding dangerous to his own ears. "It's not as if you joined the circus, is it?"

"He knew that I was putting myself at risk," Anya said softly. "He thought I was doing it because I was too foolish to see the potential consequences of my decision. By which he didn't mean an eight-month stint in a dungeon. He assumed I would get killed."

Tarek thought of his own father, and the expectations he had placed on his heir. "He does not have much faith in you."

Anya smiled again, edgily. "The responsibility of bearing his name comes with a requirement to help others. And surely the best way to do that is in controlled circumstances, like a surgical theater. Emergency rooms can be rowdy enough. But to risk myself in the middle of other people's wars? He disdained these choices."

"Surely the risk makes the help you give that much more critical."

"I would love to sit here, agree with you, and puff myself up with self-righteousness." Anya's gaze was direct again, then. And this time it made his chest feel tight. "But it wasn't as if I felt some glorious calling to immerse myself in dangerous places, all to help people who needed it. I know the difference, because every single one of my colleagues felt that call. But not me."

"Then why?" Tarek asked, though he had the distinct impression he did not wish to know the answer. The twist of her lips told him so. "Why did you do it?"

Anya let out a faint sort of laugh, and looked away. She loosened her grip on her own fingers. "You have no idea what it's like. The pressure. The endless stress. The expectation that no matter what's happening in your own life, or to you physically, you will always operate with the total recall of everything you learned in medical school, be able to apply it, and never make a mistake. It's a high-wire act and there is no soft landing. It's day in, day out, brutal and grueling and all-consuming. And that's just the emergency room."

"As it happens," Tarek said quietly, "I might have some idea."

Her gaze slid back to him. "All that gets worse in a war zone. You have to do all of the same things faster and more accurately, with or without any support staff. All while knowing that any moment you could be caught up in the crossfire."

"You say you were not called to do these things, but you did them," Tarek pointed out. "Maybe the call you were looking for does not feel the way you imagine it will."

He knew that well enough. Because it was one thing to spend a life preparing for duty, honoring the call from his own blood and history. And it was something else to stand beside the body of a man who had been both his King and his father, and know that no matter how he might wish to grieve, he had instead to step into his new role. At once.

Then to do it.

Even in the face of his own brother's betrayal.

"I didn't have a death wish, necessarily," Anya told him, as if she was confessing her sins to him. "But I took risks the others didn't because deep down? I wanted something to happen to me."

He felt everything in him sharpen. "You mean you wished to be hurt?"

"Just enough." She looked haunted, hectic. He could see how she was breathing, hard and deep, making her whole chest heave. "Just so I wouldn't have to do it anymore."

"Courage is not the absence of fear, Anya," Tarek said, his gaze on hers, something hot and hard inside his chest. "It is not somehow rising above self-pity, wild imaginings, or bitter fantasies that you might be struck down into oblivion so you need not handle what is before you. I'm afraid courage is simply doing what you must, no matter how you happen to feel about it."

She sat back in her chair, her eyes much too bright. "Thank you," she whispered. "But I know exactly how much of a coward I am. Because I also know that there was a part of me that actually enjoyed eight months of rest. When no one could possibly expect me to pick up a stethoscope or try to make them feel better. I got to rest for the first time since I entered a premed program at Cornell."

Tarek was riveted, despite himself. When surely, he ought to wrest control of this conversation. Of her. Instead, his blood was a roar within him. And he could not seem to make himself look away.

"So, yes," Anya said softly. "I will marry you. But I have two conditions."

"Conditions," he repeated, provoked that easily. He made a show of blinking, as if he had never heard the word. "It is almost as if I am any man at all. Not the King of Alzalam. Upon whom no conditions have ever been applied."

"If you want a press release, there are conditions."

Tarek tamped down the sudden surge of his temper, telling himself that this was good. If she'd leaped into this, heedless and foolish, surely it would have been proof that she would be a terrible queen. He could not have that.

"Very well then," he said, through gritted teeth. "Tell me what it is you want. I promised I would give it to you."

"First," Anya said, searching his face, "promise me that I will never have to be a doctor."

"Done. And the second condition?"

He was fascinated to watch her cheeks heat up again. "Well," she said, her voice stilted. "It's a bit more…indelicate."

"Was there delicacy in these discussions?" His voice was sardonic. "I must have missed it."

"I want a night," she blurted out. "With you. To see whether or not…"

And Tarek did not plan to ever admit, even to himself, what it cost him to simply…wait.

When everything inside him was too hot, too intent. Too hungry.

Anya cleared her throat. "To see whether or not this is real chemistry. Or if it's because you were the first man I interacted with outside that cell. I…need to know the difference."

A good man might have pointed out that it seemed likely this was all yet another attempt at self-immolation on her part.

But then, Tarek had no problem being her fire.

"Come," he said, reaching out his hand as he had at the mouth of the prison cell, his gaze hot enough to burn. "Let us find out."

CHAPTER SIX

A WISE WOMAN would have questioned her own sanity, Anya thought. Or certainly her motives.

Wise or foolish, Anya hadn't stopped trembling for some time. Deep inside, where every part of her that shook was connected to the heat that seemed to blaze between her and Tarek, and that aching, slick fire between her legs.

She told herself that what mattered was that it all made sense in her own head.

He wanted a queen. A press release and the performance that would go with it.

And she wanted a different life. With the clarity she'd gotten in the dungeon, Anya knew she could never go back. Not to who she'd been, destroying herself with stress, locking herself away when the panic hit, terrified that she was moments away from being found out for the fraud she truly was. She couldn't keep moving from one way of administering medicine to another, until she started hoping that mortar fire might take her out and save her from her inability to walk away from the life she'd spent so long—too long—building.

Maybe if she was the Queen of a faraway country she could do more good than she'd ever managed as a doctor riddled with her own guilt and shame.

And somehow, all of that seemed tied together with Tarek himself. Not the King, but the man.

Too beautiful. Too intense.

And unless she was mistaken, feeling all the same fire that she was.

Anya didn't want to be mistaken. But she also wanted to feel *alive*.

She didn't need a primer on all the ways it could go badly for her to marry this man on a whim. All the ways it could turn out to be a far worse prison than the one she'd just left.

She wanted one night. One night, just the two of them, to see.

"No kings, no queens," she said, looking up at him as he rose to stand there before her, his hand extended. "Just a woman and a man, until dawn."

"Come," he said again, with all that power and confidence. Heat and promise.

Anya took her time getting to her feet, not sure her legs would hold her up. But they did. And as she had hours ago, she reached over and slid her hand into his.

Once more, the heat punched through her. She pulled in a swift breath, but that only made it worse. His hand was too hard. His grip was too sure.

And the way he watched her, those dark eyes fixed on her, made her quiver.

She expected him to bear her off again, marching her through the palace with the same courtly formality he'd shown earlier.

Instead, Tarek pulled her closer to him.

With an offhanded display of strength that had her sprawling against the hard wall of his chest, and gasping a bit while she did it.

Because it had been one thing to say she wanted this. And something else to be so close to another person.

To him.

Her pulse skyrocketed as she gazed up at him. If it was possible, Tarek was even more beautiful up close. Even more compelling. He smoothed his hands over her head, sliding that scarf out of his way.

And she watched, transfixed, as he pulled a long, glossy strand of her hair between two fingers. Looking down at it, very seriously, as if it held the mysteries of the universe.

Then he shifted that look to her.

"Tarek—" she began.

His hard mouth curved. "I like my name in your mouth. But I have other priorities."

Then he bent his head and put that stern mouth of his on hers.

Everything inside of Anya, all that fire and need, exploded.

Tarek gripped her head, he angled his jaw, and then he swept her away.

His kiss was a hard claiming. He possessed her, challenged her and dared her. Anya surged forward, pressing her palms harder against the glory that was his hard chest as if she could disappear into all his heat.

And she kissed him back, pouring everything she had into it. Into him.

Again and again.

He made a low, gloriously male sound, then tore his mouth from hers.

"No," Anya breathed, heedless and needy. "Don't stop."

He laughed. Deep, dark, rich. It rolled through her, setting her alight all over again.

Anya felt swollen and desperate straight through, and he was still laughing.

"Order me around, Doctor," he suggested, his voice moving inside her as if it was a part of her. As if it was the sun, even now, in the dark of night. "Tell me what to do and see how that works for you."

But before she could try, mostly to see what he would do, Tarek bent slightly to sweep her into his arms.

Anya knew that none of this made sense. That she should have left with the American ambassador when she'd had the chance. That she certainly shouldn't have exposed herself to this man, telling him secrets she'd never breathed to another living soul.

Yet she had.

What was another vulnerability to add to the list? Maybe she was lucky she hadn't become a psychiatrist. She doubted she would enjoy knowing the inner workings of her own mind. Not when there was a king gazing down at her, his expression stern and possessive, sending a spiral of delight all the way through her.

Maybe, finally, it was time to stop thinking altogether. And to let herself feel instead.

Because she already knew what it was like to sit frozen in the dark. Literally.

Tonight, Anya intended to shine. And live. And feel everything—every last drop of sensation she was capable of feeling. Every touch, every sigh, every searing bit of flame she could hoard and call her own.

It took her a moment to realize that Tarek was moving. His powerful body was all around her, those arms of his holding her aloft as if she weighed little more than a notion. The granite wall of his chest. The tempting hollow at the base of his throat. His scent, a faint hint of smoke and what she assumed gold might smell like, warmed through and made male.

She assumed he would carry her off to his bed, wherever that was in this sprawling place, but instead he headed out through the grand, windowed doors that led outside. Anya caught a glimpse of the lights of the old city, gleaming soft against the desert night. Then he was setting her down, and it took her a moment to get her bearings, to find herself out on one of the palace's many balconies.

This one was made for comfort. He placed her on one of many low, bright couches, ringed all around with torches, and a canopy far above. There was a thick rug tossed across the ground at her feet and lanterns scattered across the table, making her think of long-ago stories she'd read as a child.

Tarek stood before her, gazing down at her as if she was the spoils of the war he'd fought, and he intended to fully immerse himself in the plunder.

Her entire body reacted to that thought as if she'd been doused in kerosene. She was too hot. She had too many clothes on. She was *burning alive*.

Looking at him was like a panic attack, except inside out. Anya's heart pounded. She could feel herself grow far too warm. And she felt a little dizzy, a little unsure.

But what was laced through all of that wasn't fear.

There was only him.

And how deeply, how wantonly and impossibly, she wanted him.

As she watched, Tarek began to remove those robes of his, casting them aside in a flutter of ivory and gold. He kept going until he stood before her, magnificently naked.

And when he made no move toward her, she felt a moment's confusion—

But then, as her gaze moved over his body, roped with muscle and impossibly powerful, she found the red, raised scars. One crossed the flat slab of his left pectoral muscle. Another cut deep across his torso, all along one half of the V that marked where his ridged wonder of an abdomen gave way to all the relentless masculinity beneath. Those were the biggest, most shocking scars—but there were more. Smaller ones, crisscrossing here and there.

Anya realized she was holding her breath.

And she thought he realized it too, because with no more than a simmering look, he turned so she could see the ones on his back.

"Your scars," she whispered.

"They came in the night like the cowards they were," Tarek told her, slowly turning back to face her. "But let me assure you, their wounds were far greater than mine."

"Wounds are wounds," Anya said. And she wondered what lay beneath his. What it must have felt like for him, with his own brother involved in the plot against him. "And the marks we carry on our skin is the least of it, I think."

"Perhaps." He inclined his head in that way of his. So arrogant, every inch of him the absolute ruler he was, that she didn't know whether to scream or launch herself at him. "But what matters is that I won."

Anya had spent hours with this man by now. And had thought only of herself. Rightly so, maybe, given what had happened to her.

But she thought of his words from earlier. *Tell*

me your secrets, and I will show you my scars. She thought of the fact that he hid them in the first place.

That he clearly had no intention of discussing his *feelings*, God forbid.

And it occurred to her, in a flash that felt a lot like need, that though he stood before her, the very picture of male arrogance, what he was showing her was vulnerability.

This was how this man, this King who had fought off his enemies and protected his throne and his people with his own hands, showed anything like vulnerability.

Anya understood, then. If she showed him softness, it would insult him. If she cried for the insult done to his beautiful body, she would do nothing but court his temper.

Tarek was not a soft man. And he did not require her tears.

So she responded the only way she could.

She flowed forward, moving from the edge of the cushion where she sat to her knees before him. She tipped her head back to look up at him, catching the harshness of his gaze. Matching it with her own.

Bracing her hands on either side of his hips, Anya took the hard, proud length of him deep into her mouth.

He tasted like rain. A hint of salt, that driving heat, and beneath it, something fresh and bright and male.

She had never tasted anything so good in her life.

Anya sucked him in as far as she could, then

wrapped her hand around the base of him to make up for what she couldn't fit in her mouth.

And then, using her mouth and her hands together and his hard length like steel, she taught herself what it was to live again.

His hands fisted in her hair. Anya thrilled at the twin pulls *this close* to pain that arrowed straight to where she ached the most. Sensations stormed through her as she took him deep, then played with the thick, wide head, using her tongue. And then suction. And anything else that felt good.

He groaned, and that sent bolt after bolt of that wildfire sensation streaking through her body to lodge itself in her soft heat, where it pulsed.

Tarek was muttering, dirty words in several languages, and Anya loved that, too.

She wanted all of him. She wanted, desperately, for him to flood her mouth so she could swallow him whole. So she could take some part of him—of this—inside her and hold on to it, forever.

And this time, she was the one who groaned when he pulled her away from him. It took her a few jagged breaths to recognize that the man who looked down at her then was not the King. Not the indulgent monarch.

He looked like a man.

A man at the end of his rope. And he was somehow more beautiful for that wildness.

Tarek hauled her up to her feet.

"You will be the death of me," he growled at her.

"But a good death," Anya replied, though her mouth felt like his, because he was all she could taste. "Isn't that the point?"

"I have no intention of dying," Tarek told her fiercely. His hands were busy, and she felt too limp, too ravaged by lust and need, to do anything but stand there as he stripped her of her tunic, her trousers, her silky underthings. "Certainly not before I had tasted every inch of you, *habibti*."

And when he bore her down to the soft cushions behind her, they were both gloriously undressed at last.

Anya felt as if she'd been waiting a lifetime for this. For him.

At first it was almost like a fight, as they each wrestled to taste more. To consume each other whole.

She kissed his scars, one after the next, until he flipped her over and set about his own tasting. Each breast. Her nipples. The trail he made himself down the length of her abdomen, until he could take a long, deep drink from between her legs.

But even though she bucked against him, on the edge of shattering, he only laughed. That dark, rich sound that seemed to pulse in her. Then he nipped at the inside of her thigh.

"Not so fast, *habibti*," he said, climbing back up her body. "I wish to watch you come apart. So deep inside you that neither one of us can breathe. So there can be no mistake that no matter what else happens in the course of my reign, no matter what we find in this practical arrangement of ours, we will always have this."

And before she could react to that, he twisted his hips and drove himself, hard and huge, deep inside of her.

Anya simply...snapped.

She arched up, shattering all around him with that single stroke that was almost too much. Almost too deep.

She rocked herself against him, over and over, as the storm of it took her apart, shaking her again and again until she forgot who she was.

And as she came back, she was gradually aware that Tarek waited, smoke and gold and dark eyes trained on her face, as if he was drinking in every last moment.

He was still so hard. Still so deep inside her she could feel him when she breathed. He braced himself above her, that beautiful predator's gaze trained on her. And the sight of all that barely contained ferocity above her while he was planted within her made the heat inside her flare all over again.

"This is not a hallucination brought on by a prison cell," he told her, his voice no more than a growl.

"No," she agreed, breathlessly. She wrapped her legs around him because she knew, somehow, that she needed to hold on tight. "This is who we are."

And Tarek smiled at her, though it was a fierce thing, all teeth and sensual promise.

Only then did he begin to move.

It was like coming home.

He wasn't gentle. She wasn't sweet. It was a clashing of bodies, pleasure so intense it made her scream.

Tarek pounded into her, his mouth against her neck. They flipped over once and she found herself astride him. She braced herself against his chest as she worked her hips to get *more*, to ride that line between pleasure and pain when it was all part of the same glory.

To make them one, to make them *this*.

Then they flipped again and he was on his knees, lifting her so he could wrap his arms around her hips and let her arch back as she wished. She did, lifting her breasts to his mouth for him to feast upon while he worked her against him, over and over.

Until she couldn't tell if he pounded into her or she surged against him. It was all one.

Finally, Tarek gathered her beneath him again. He reached down between them while still he surged into her, that same furious pace, and pinched the place where she needed him most.

Hard enough to make her scream.

And while she screamed for him, explode.

Anya sobbed as he kept pounding into her, again and again, aware that she felt like she was flying. Like she was finally free.

She felt him empty himself inside her with a shout as they both catapulted straight into the eye of the storm they'd made.

And shook together, until it was done.

For a long while, Anya knew very little.

Slowly, she became aware of herself again, but barely. And only when Tarek shifted, pulling out of the clutch of her body, but moving only far enough to stretch out beside her. He shifted her to his chest and she breathed there while the night air washed over her body, cooling her down slowly.

Anya thought she really ought to spend some time analyzing what had just happened. If it was possible to analyze…all that. She should consider what to do now. Now that she knew. Now that there was no going back from that knowing.

But that felt far too ambitious.

Instead, she rested her cheek against his chest. She could feel the ridge of his scar and beneath it, the thunder of his heart. It felt a lot like poetry. She watched the torches set at intervals around them dance and flicker. From where they lay, stretched out on the wide sofa, she could see the tallest spires of the city in the distance. Rising up above them as if they were keeping watch while the desert breeze played lazily with the canopy far above.

Anya was wrecked. Undone.

And she had never felt so alive, so fully herself, in all her days.

"Well?" came Tarek's voice, from above and beneath her at once.

He sounded different, she thought, as she shifted so she could look at him. And though he gazed at her with all his usual arrogance, there was an indulgent quirk to his fine, sensual lips.

She hungered for him, all over again, her body heating anew.

It should have scared her, these postprison appetites. But she knew that what charged through her was nothing so simple as fear.

Fear left her sprawled out on bathroom floors, gasping for her breath. It didn't make her feel sunlight in a desert night, or as if she'd discovered wings she'd never known were there. Fear reduced her into nothing but a set of symptoms she couldn't think through. It created nothing, taught her nothing, and never left her anything like sated.

Anya had never considered it before, but fear was simple.

What stormed in her because of Tarek, *with* Tarek, was complicated. Possibly insane, yes. But there were too many layers in it for her to count. Too many contradictions and connections. Scar tissue and the stars above, and that delirious heat, too.

"And if I say that I have never been so disappointed?" she asked, though she couldn't keep herself from smiling.

His smile did not change his face, it made him more of what he was. *Like a hawk*, she thought, as she had from the first. He made her shiver with a single look. But he also held her there, tight against his body, as if he would never let go.

"Then I will call you a liar," he said, dark and sure. "Which is no way to begin a marriage, I think."

He waited, that fierce gaze of his on her. Stark and certain. And yet Anya knew that all she needed to do was roll away from him. Thank him, perhaps, and he would let her go.

She could be back in the States before she knew it. Back to whatever her life was going to look like, on the other side of this. And by *this* she wasn't sure she meant the dungeon so much as the fact she'd finally admitted all those dark, secret things in her heart. She had finally said them out loud.

How could she go back from that?

"Be my Queen, Anya," Tarek urged her, his voice a dark, royal command. She could feel it in every part of her, particularly when he shifted so he could bend over her once more, bringing his mouth almost close enough to hers. Almost. "Marry me."

He was holding her tight, yet she felt set free.

Whatever else happened, surely that was what mattered.

"I take it you want a real marriage," she said as if the idea was distasteful to her, when it was nothing of the kind. "Not one of those 'for show' ones royals supposedly have. For the people and the press releases and what have you."

And this time, she could feel his smile against her mouth. "I will insist."

"All right then," Anya muttered, trying to sound

grumpy when she was smiling too. "I suppose I'll marry you, Tarek."

From captive to Queen, in the course of one evening.

It made her dizzy.

Then he did, when he took her mouth in a kiss so possessive she almost thought it might leave a bruise.

Anya wished it would.

And she told herself, as she melted against him all over again, that Tarek might be a king. That the King might have his practical reasons for this most bizarre of marriages. That the man who had fought his own family and wore their marks on his skin might have all kinds of reasons for the things he did, and he might not have told her half of them.

But that she was the one claiming him, even so.

CHAPTER SEVEN

LIFE IN THE DUNGEON was slow. One day crawled by, then the next, on and into eternity, every one of them the same. The world outside the windows turned. Changed. Seasons came and went, but the dungeon stayed the same.

But after Anya agreed to marry Tarek, everything sped up.

"First," said Ahmed, the King's dignified, intimidating aide and personal assistant in one, a few days after she and Tarek had come to terms, "I believe there is the issue of press releases to local and international outlets alike."

"Oh," Anya said after a moment, staring back at the man. "You mean real ones."

"Indeed, madam. They would otherwise be somewhat ineffective, would they not?"

She was seated in the King's vast office, trying to look appropriately queenly. Trying also not to second-guess herself and the choices she'd made. But she'd snuck a look at Tarek then. "We wouldn't want that."

And she'd taken it as a personal victory when the stern, uncompromising King of Alzalam, sitting like a forbidding statue behind his appropriately commanding desk, had visibly bit back a smile.

If Anya was fully honest she didn't really want to face the outside world. Every time she thought of her overly full mobile, she shuddered. But she also knew that as much as she might have liked to do absolutely nothing but lose herself in the passion she had never felt before in her life, that slick and sweet glory only Tarek seemed to provide, that wasn't the bargain they'd made.

She was going to have to face the real world sooner or later, she reasoned. That might as well be under the aegis of the palace, so they could control the message. And help shelter her from the response.

"Timing is an issue," Tarek said after a moment, no trace of laughter in his voice. "We would not wish to suggest that there was any romance conducted while you were more or less in chains."

"A king romancing a captive can really only occur within a certain window," Anya agreed merrily. "Lest we all forget ourselves and start fretting about upsetting power dynamics."

"No one who has met you, Doctor," Tarek murmured then, "would have the slightest doubt where the power lay."

And though Ahmed looked at her as if that was meant to be an insult, Anya knew it wasn't.

Because when they weren't discussing media campaigns, wedding arrangements, or thorny issues of which family members to invite—what with her father being her father, and a number of Tarek's relatives being in jail for attempting to kill him—they were exploring that fire that only seemed to blaze hotter between them.

Tarek, it turned out, hid a sensualist of the highest order beneath his stern exterior.

"You are always hungry," he mused one night as Anya happily polished off yet another feast. They'd taken to eating in one of the private rooms in her apartments, the two of them sitting cross-legged on the floor where it was far easier to reach for each other when a different sort of hunger took control.

She paused in the act of pressing her linen napkin to her lips, waiting for a comment like that to turn dark. For Tarek to make her feel bad the way her father always had, with snide little remarks like knives.

But instead, he smiled. "I take pleasure in sating each and every one of your hunger pangs."

And he made good on that at once, tugging the napkin from her fingers and laying her out flat before him on the scattered pillows. He drew the hem of the long, lustrous skirt she wore up the length of her legs. Then he lifted her hips and settled his mouth at her core, licking his way into her molten heat.

Only when he had her bucking against him,

shattering and sobbing out his name, did Tarek sit back again. Then sedately returned to his dinner, merely lifting an arrogant brow when she cursed him weakly, lying there amongst the pillows in complete disarray.

"I do not wait for my dessert," he told her, as if he was discussing matters of state. "If I wish to indulge myself, I do so immediately."

"As you wish, Your Majesty," she panted.

It took Anya a full week to face up to the reality of what awaited her on her mobile, much less the repeated requests for appointments with the American embassy. Not to mention the press releases—more a press junket, Ahmed informed her solemnly—that she'd promised Tarek.

A week to face her new reality and another week to decide that she was well enough prepared to handle it. Or if not prepared, not likely to suffer irreparable harm when subjecting herself to reporters and their intrusive questions.

She did the biggest interviews first, sitting in a room of the palace that seemed like an anachronism. It was tucked away next to an ancient courtyard that a small plaque announced had existed in one form or another even before the palace had been fully built. Truly medieval, yet it invited any who entered to breathe deep and forget about the passage of time.

But inside the media room, it was very clear what century Anya was in. It was all monitors and lights, cameras and green screens. The palace's senior press

secretary ushered her through the roster of engage-
ments, where all Anya had to do was tell her story.

And more critically, her reasons for remaining in
Alzalam now she'd been freed.

"It's hard to imagine what would keep you there,"
said one anchorwoman. She wrinkled her brow as if
in concern—or tried. "Surely most people in your
position would try to get home as quickly as possible."

"I don't know that many people in my position,"
Anya replied. She reminded herself to smile, be-
cause if she didn't, people asked why she was *so mad*.
"Captured, held, then released into a royal palace.
Maybe I think that having spent so much time in
the kingdom, it might be nice to explore it a little."

And then, on the heels of a morning filled with
interviews from all over the world, she marched herself back to her rooms, dug her phone out of her bag,
and forced herself to deal with all of her messages
and voice mails.

It took hours. But when she was done, she felt
both more emotional than she'd anticipated, and
less panicky. A good number of the voice mail messages were from an array of journalists, some of
whom she'd already spoken to. A few friends had
called over the past eight months, claiming they only
wanted to hear her voice and letting her know they'd
been thinking of her during her ordeal. She took a
surprising amount of pleasure in discovering that a

bulk of her email was, as always, online catalogs she couldn't remember shopping from in the first place.

It made her feel as if, no matter what, life went on.

Better still, Anya felt somewhat better about the fact she still hadn't called her father, because he had neither written nor called her. Not once in all the time she'd been held in the dungeon. And, of course, not before that either, because he hadn't approved of her wasting her time in an aid organization when she could do something of much greater status and import.

Maybe it told her something about herself—or him—that she felt a bit triumphant when she finally dialed the number of the house she'd grown up in. She knew the number by heart, still, even though the house and the number attached to it hadn't been hers in a long while. Since long before she'd left it, in fact.

She stood in her elegant suite, looking out the window as yet another desert sky stretched out before her. Impossibly blue to the horizon and beyond. Looking out at so much sky, so much sand, made her feel as if she was just as expansive. As if, should she gather up enough courage, she might run through these windows, out to her terrace, and launch herself straight into the wind. Then fly.

It made her heart ache in a good way.

Anya had never felt that way in the excruciatingly tidy Victorian house on a Seattle hill where her father still lived. More care had been put into the gardens than her feelings. She had grown up guilty. Because she barely recalled her own mother. Because she was forever disturbing her father. Because she didn't usually like the women he married and presented to her as so much furniture. Because they mostly didn't care for her, either—and as the window between her age and the current stepmother's age narrowed, she felt even guiltier at how relieved she was to stop pretending.

She had left for college and had never returned for more than a brief visit over the holidays. She would have said that she barely remembered the place that her father's cleaners kept so pristine that it was sometimes hard to believe people actually lived there. Even when she'd been one of them.

But she could see it all too clearly, now.

As if all this time away forced her to look at it face on, at last. Not the house itself, but the fact it had never been a home.

The dungeon beneath this palace, hewn of cold, hard stone, had been cozier. Happier, even. She had catapulted herself out of her father's house as quickly as she could. The urgency to get it behind her—the kind of urgency the anchorwoman thought Anya should feel about Alzalam—had guided her every move after she'd graduated high school. But it wasn't as if she'd ever made herself a home elsewhere.

She'd been moving from place to place ever since, concentrating on school, then her job, then how much she hated her job. She'd never settled anywhere, she'd only endured wherever she'd found herself.

Until the dungeon had settled on her.

First she'd despaired, as anyone would. Then she'd tried to make someone tell her how long she could expect to be left there. But after the despair and the bargaining, there was only time.

When she'd told Tarek that prison had been a kind of holiday, she'd meant it. Now she had the unsettling realization that it had also felt a whole lot more like a home than any other place she'd ever lived. No expectations. No demands.

Just time.

What was Anya supposed to do with that?

"Oh," came the breathy voice of her latest stepmother when she picked up the phone. For a moment, Anya couldn't remember her name. Or more precisely, she remembered a name, but wasn't sure it was the right one. It had been eight months, after all. "Anya. My goodness. You've been all over the news."

Charisma, Anya thought then, recognizing her voice. That was this stepmother's name. It was, of course, a deeply ironic name for a creature with all the natural charisma of a signpost. But Charisma was young. Anya's exact age, if she was remembering right, which said all kinds of things about Dr. Preston Turner that Anya preferred not to think about too closely.

Charisma was not smart, according to Anya's father. He liked to say this in Charisma's hearing, and she always proved his hypothesis to his satisfaction by giggling as if that was an endearment. Charisma was blonde in that silky way that seemed to require endless flipping of the straw-colored mass of it over one shoulder, then the other. Her hobbies involved numerous appointments at beauty salons and sitting by the pool in a microscopic bikini.

Charisma also managed to make it sound as if Anya had gone on the news in a deliberate attempt to provoke her father. As if she was indulging in attention-seeking behavior by telling her story.

Anya didn't have the heart to tell this woman that she'd given up on attempting to get Preston Turner's attention a long time ago. Or that she should do the same.

"I would prefer not to be on the news," Anya said, proud of how steady she kept her voice. With a hint of self-deprecation, even. "But apparently you become a person of interest when you're snatched up in a foreign country, thrown into prison, and then disappear for eight months. I don't see the appeal myself."

Charisma made a breathy, sighing sort of sound. "Your father's at the hospital," she said. "Do you want me to tell him that you called? He's very upset."

"He's been worried about me?" Anya asked, in complete disbelief.

"There have been a lot of questions," Charisma hedged. "And you know how your father is. When he's at the country club he really doesn't like to be approached or recognized. So."

"So," Anya echoed. She did not point out that the entire purpose of her father's snooty country club was to be recognized. What would be the point? "What I think you're telling me, Charisma, is that my imprisonment was an inconvenience."

"It was just all those questions," her stepmother said airily. "He would have appreciated it if you'd given him a little warning, maybe."

Anya's good intentions deserted her. "Funnily enough, they didn't offer me the opportunity to make a lot of phone calls," she said, and her voice was not even. It was inarguably sharp. "I was thrown in a dungeon. And then kept there, without any contact with the outside world, for the better part of the year."

"Well, I'm not going to tell him *that*." Charisma laughed. "You know how he gets. You can tell him that if you want."

"I'll go ahead and do that," Anya said, already furious at herself for showing emotion. When she knew Charisma would report it back to her father and it would only give him more ammunition to disdain her. "The next time he calls."

Which would be never.

After she ended the call she stayed where she was, standing still in the bright glare of the desert sun, trying to make sense of all the competing feelings that stormed around inside her.

She could feel that sharp pain in her chest, that knotted thing pulling tight again. Anya rubbed at it with the heel of her hand, then wheeled around, heading toward that bright, happy room Tarek had showed her that first day. She liked how dizzy the light made her, still. She liked that if it became too much, she could go out and dunk herself in that infinity pool. It soothed her to float there, folding her arms over the lip of it while she gazed out across the city to the desert, always waiting beyond.

Before now, Anya had always considered herself an ocean sort of person. She'd always love the sea, its immensity and pull. She'd grown up in a city surrounded by water, and had imagined she would always live where she could see it, or access it, because it was what she knew. But she hadn't.

And something about the desert stirred her, deep inside. It was like the ocean inside out. It was a reminder, always, that no matter what was happening to her, something far greater and more powerful than petty human concerns stood just there. Watching. Waiting. And perfectly capable of wiping it all away.

She supposed other people might not find that comforting.

But then, when had Anya ever been like other people? If she was anything like other people, she might have remained a doctor in the emergency room of her busy hospital in Houston, Texas. She might have felt called to medicine like so many of her fellow doctors. Or even called to money and prestige, like her father.

Instead, she found as the days passed that becoming a queen gave her far more opportunities to truly help people. Without having to run triage, check vitals, or desperately operate a crash cart.

Even thinking about those things made her blood pressure rise.

She sat down with her own aides, who showed up one day at Tarek's order. They discussed different sorts of charity work. Initiatives Anya could undertake. Both the traditional province of Alzalam queens, and new ideas about the sorts of things she, as the most untraditional Queen in the kingdom's long history, could attempt.

A month after Tarek had appeared at the door of her cell, they announced their engagement.

But they did it in the traditional Alzalam fashion.

Meaning, the announcement was made and the nation launched itself into a week-long celebration that would culminate in the wedding itself.

"Your people do not waste any time," Anya said, standing out on a balcony Tarek had told her was built for precisely this purpose. The King and his chosen bride together, waving at the cheering crowd gathered below. "What's the rush? Are you afraid the bride will change her mind?"

"Historically yes." He shot her a narrow look, laced with that amusement she had come to crave. Because she knew it was only hers. "Many brides were kidnapped from an enemy tribe, and it was always best not to leave too much time between taking her and claiming her, in case the warriors from her tribe came to collect her."

"Romantic," Anya murmured. "Practically to Western levels, really."

She was rewarded for that with the bark of his laughter.

And she was starting to get used to how deeply she craved such things. His touch. His laughter. *Him.*

Not that she dared say such things to Tarek.

It wouldn't do to throw too much emotion into their very practical arrangement. She knew that. And no matter that she found it harder and harder to pretend her feelings weren't involved.

Anya sobbed out his name regularly, but kept her feelings to herself.

Just as she decided it was best not to tell this man of stone that sometimes, her own panic dropped her to the floor. Because that might not only involve emotions—Tarek's response to such a weakness might spark an attack.

She had spent hours in fittings over the past month, as packs of the kingdom's finest seamstresses descended upon her, determined to make sure that everything she wore—whether traditional or Western, depending on which day of the wedding week it was—reflected the glory of the King.

"And accents your own beauty of course, my lady," the head seamstress had murmured at one point, after there had been quite a lot of carrying on about Tarek and the honor due him from the women assembled in the room.

With more than a few speculative looks thrown her way, not all of them as friendly as they could have been.

But she understood.

"Of course," Anya had replied. "But I must only be an accent. It is the King who must shine."

That had changed the mood in the room. Considerably.

And it was not until later that Anya—who would once have ripped off heads if anyone had suggested she was an *accent* to a man—realized that somehow…she meant that.

The realization hit her like a blow as she stood in her glorious shower, and when her heart kicked in, she froze. She expected the panic to rush at her, to take her to the shower floor. She expected to sit there, naked and wet and miserable, until it finished with her.

But the panic didn't come.

No nausea, no hyperventilating, no worries that she might aspirate her own saliva and choke while unable to help herself.

The hot water rained down upon her. Anya pressed the heel of her hand into that tightness in her solar plexus, hard.

But still, though she could feel that she was *agitated*, there was no panic.

"Because I chose this," she whispered out loud. "I chose him."

It was hardly a thread of sound, her voice. She could barely hear herself over the sound of the water.

But it rang in her, loud and true, and kept ringing long after she left the shower and dried herself off.

The night they announced their engagement,

Tarek did not eat dinner with her the way he'd been doing, too caught up was he in matters of state. Anya ate alone, enjoying her solitude now that it was not enforced. She read a book. She caught up with her far-flung friends, many of whom could not make it to this remote kingdom on such short notice, no matter how they wished they could. She let herself…be part of the world again.

After she ate, she sat outside. She found she couldn't get enough of the desert evenings. The sunsets were spectacular, a riot of colors that never failed to make her catch her breath. And even in the dark, she could feel the desert itself, stretching on and on in all directions, almost as if it called to her. She wrapped herself up in a blanket when she grew cold and stayed tucked up under the heaters, watching the magical old city bloom as the lights came on. Her aides had taken her on a guided tour of the narrow streets, the ancient buildings stacked high, and the more she saw of it, the more she loved it.

A mystery around every corner. History in every step. And wherever she turned, the people who smiled at her and called out their support of Tarek. Making her foolish heart swell every time she heard it.

They were not the only ones who adored him.

She didn't think she fell asleep, but one moment she was gazing out at the city and the next, he was there. As if she'd conjured him from the spires and lights that spread out behind him.

Anya smiled, then studied that face of his, sensual and harsh at once. "What's the matter?"

She was learning how to read him now, this man she would marry in seven days. He was always fierce. He was always, without question, the King. But there were different levels of ferocity in him, and tonight it seemed…darker.

Something inside her curled up tight in a kind of warning. The knot inside her grew three sizes.

But she kept her gaze on Tarek, and ignored them both.

"Nothing is the matter," he told her, standing there at the foot of the chaise where she was curled up. In a voice that was little more than a growl. "Save my own weakness."

"You have a weakness?" Anya asked lightly. "Quick, tell me what it is, so I might exploit it."

Tarek didn't laugh at that. His hard mouth did not betray the faintest curve. Anya ordered herself not to panic, or note that it felt too much like loss.

Or worse, ask herself how she could feel the things she felt after so little time.

"I spent the night in tense negotiations," Tarek said, staring down at her as if he couldn't quite make sense of her. Or as if Anya had *done something* to him. "It is the kind of diplomacy that I abhor. Snide remarks masquerading as communication. All employed by men who would never last a moment on any kind of real battlefield. Still, these things are part of what I am called to do. As such, they deserve my full attention."

"I'm sure you give everything your full attention."

As it happened, Anya had become something like obsessed with the force of Tarek's full attention. With the sorts of things he could do with all that *focus*. Her body shivered into readiness at once, her nipples forming hard peaks, her belly tightening, and the soft, yearning place where she wanted him most like fire.

The ways she hungered for this man never ceased to surprise her. But the way he looked at her now did. As if she'd betrayed him in some way.

"The only thing I could think about was you," he told her, his voice a rough scrape against the dark.

It was not a declaration of feelings. It was an accusation.

An outrage.

For a moment, Anya froze, feeling as if he'd kicked her. That terrible knot grew teeth. But in the next moment, she breathed out. And again, as she had the night he showed her his scars, Anya understood that this was not something she could laugh away. She couldn't show him her first reaction. Once again, it was not softness or emotion he needed.

Maybe, something in her whispered, *all that medical training was not to keep your cool in an emergency room. Maybe it was so you could stare down a king no matter his mood, and be what he needs. Whether or not he knows how to ask for it.*

Not because she was losing herself in him, as one article she'd read about herself tonight had suggested. But because he wasn't simply a man, who a woman might argue with about domestic arrangements or respect or any number of things.

His people needed him to rule above all else. They had told her so themselves, out in the winding streets of this age-old city. And if she wanted to marry him, to be his Queen as well as his woman, she needed to support the King first.

Only once the ruler was handled could she tend to the man.

Because she was the only one who got both.

"You're welcome," Anya said, neither gently nor particularly apologetically.

He blinked at that, a slow show of arrogant disbelief that made her pulse pick up. "I beg your pardon?"

She didn't quite shrug. "Tedious negotiations with terrible people, you say? How lucky you must feel to know that I'll be waiting for you at the end of it." Anya nodded regally toward the foot of her chaise. "And you are even more lucky that I find myself in the mood for a king."

"Are you suggesting that it is possible that you might ever *not* be in the mood for your King?" Tarek was gazing down at her as if thunderstruck. Far better than the look that had been in his eyes before, by any reckoning. "An impossibility, surely. Or treason. You may take your pick."

"I am the Queen of this land," she told him

grandly, and only just kept herself from waving an imaginary scepter in the air between them.

Tarek's dark eyes gleamed with the fire she knew best. "Not yet, Anya. Not quite yet."

"I will be the Queen in a week, and you are trying my patience." She sniffed haughtily. "Daring to come before me and speak to me of petty concerns when you could be pleasuring me, even now."

She was sure she could see him waver there. He looked torn between the sort of erotic outrage she was going for or more of whatever temper had brought him here, too much like a storm cloud for her liking.

Anya held her breath. She waited. And she could see exactly when that hunger that never seemed to wane between them won.

"You may not like the way I worship you, my Queen," Tarek told her then, his voice deep, suggestive, and a kind of dark threat that made her shiver, happily. "But I will."

Then he fell upon her. Both of them ravenous, both of them wild.

And when he held her before him, on her hands and knees so he could take her as he liked, Anya gloried in it, in him. The impossible iron length of him was a wildfire inside her. A gorgeous catastrophe of sensation and need. She was bared entirely to his gaze and to the desert sky, vulnerable and invulnerable at once, while he surged deep inside of her and made her scream.

It was quickly becoming her favorite melody.

A song she wanted to sing out, heedless and loud, for the rest of her days.

But Tarek wasn't done. And as he pounded them both sweet again, until they were *them* again, Anya gave herself over to the only form of wedding vow she thought she'd ever need.

Again and again and again.

CHAPTER EIGHT

THE WEDDING GUESTS began to pour in the day after their announcement.

From near and far they came. Tarek welcomed in men who had fought with him, relatives and business allies, foreign heads of state and an inevitable selection of celebrities. He pretended he did not know which of his guests had spoken against him over the course of the last year and which had given him nothing but their quiet support.

But he knew. And they knew. And there was a power in the invitation to his would-be enemies, to permit them to witness how wrong they'd been about him up close. It was the logical extension of the press junket he and Anya had undertaken and Tarek could not pretend he didn't enjoy it.

There was a grand party that night to kick off the traditional week of celebrations. It was also the first opportunity for Anya to prove to the international crowd that she was not under duress. And for the people of Alzalam, that she was worthy of the role she was to assume at the end of the week.

"No pressure, then," she'd said earlier in the flippant manner only she dared employ in his presence.

Tarek had found he had to have her, in a slick rush of need, even if it meant that her aides would have to reapply all the beauty enhancements—to his mind, wholly unnecessary—that they'd used on her to prepare her for the evening.

"You will be a natural."

"Because you say so?" She had been slumped in a delicious sort of ruin where he'd left her, bonelessly draped over an ottoman in her bedchamber.

"Yes, because I say so," he'd replied. "Am I not the King?"

Anya had smiled at him, the way he liked best. Dreamy and sweet. Private.

The Anya who appeared in public never looked that soft. That was for him alone.

And as he stood in the middle of the grand party in one of the palace's ballrooms that night, Tarek found himself thinking about that smile more than he should.

Just as he thought about her more than he should, when he knew better.

Because while it turned out that the former prisoner he was marrying for purely practical reasons was remarkably good at distracting him from the things he brooded about, that didn't change the truth of them.

Like the fact he was obsessed with this woman.

Tarek knew better than that. The history of his kingdom was filled with examples of why romantic obsession was a scourge. Nothing but a curse. Many of his ancestors had been endlessly derailed by theatrics in the harem. Favorite wives seemed to lead inevitably to catastrophes—witness his former betrothed and the shame she had brought to her family. Tarek had always vowed he would never succumb to such pettiness.

He had already paid dearly for the affection he'd held for his younger brother. He could not afford a far worse blindness. He would never forgive himself.

"*Imagine my surprise,*" Anya had said at dinner one day after she'd finally got a comprehensive tour of the Royal Palace. "*I thought the dungeon was the scariest place in this building. But you actually have a harem.*"

Tarek had been feeling expansive and relaxed. He had eaten, then spread his woman out on the table. He had eaten his dessert from her skin—sweets from the sweet—before burying himself inside her to the hilt. Then they'd gone out to the tiled tub on her balcony and sunk into the hot water. He had smiled at Anya's wide eyes and scandalized tone.

"*I was raised in the harem,*" he told her. "*My mother was only the first of my father's many wives.*"

And he was not a nice man, and nothing like a good one, because he had greatly enjoyed Anya's look of horror.

"The only words we've discussed were wife and queen," she'd said then. Her shoulders had straightened with a sharp jerk, enough to make the water slosh around them. *"Wife was never plural. And neither was* queen."

"I enjoyed my childhood," Tarek had told her, reaching over to pull her to him, settling her before him, her back to his front. *"My brother and I were doted upon and when our half siblings arrived, they were, too. We all grew up together. We had maternal attention from all sides, and therefore felt that any attention we received from our father was a gift."*

He had not wanted to think about those years. When he and Rafiq had been so close. When it would have seemed laughable to him that anything could ever change that.

Even now, he sometimes forgot what had happened and thought to call his brother. Only to remember it all over again, with a sickening sort of lurch.

Anya's shoulders were no longer braced for an attack. She'd softened against him, and he liked that better.

"It's so hard to imagine that he could grow up and...do what he did," she said quietly.

Tarek tensed, and hated that she could feel it. *"When it comes to my brother, I do not imagine anything but his prison sentence."*

And his voice was so forbidding he could actually

watch her respond to it. Her shoulders had risen all over again. Her breath went shallow.

He told himself he did not, could not mind it. His brother had no place here. Childhood memories were one thing, but he would have no…*imagining.*

"*I think you would love the harem,*" he had continued after a moment. He'd tried to sound relaxed again, looking over her head toward the city before them. The sky above, the lights below. And Anya between. It made something in him…settle. "*It would certainly be one way to make friends in the kingdom.*"

He'd wondered if she would nurse her upset. If she would act as if he'd bruised her—

But this was Anya.

All she did was twist around to glare at him as if his brother had never been mentioned.

"*That, right there, is why I have no intention of filling my harem with all the wives I can support, though I certainly could. It is not worth all the fighting. The jealousy, the petty attacks, the attempts at power grabs.*" He'd shaken his head, thinking of those years. Thinking of his father's wives, not Rafiq. "*My father always acted as if he was unaware of such things, but I've never seen greater personal viciousness than I did then. It was never directed at me, but that didn't mean I didn't see it.*"

"*Thank you for this lesson on the historical use of harems here,*" Anya had said darkly. "*I have no de-*

sire to be in one, thank you. I would rather become a neurosurgeon."

"*The same accuracy and skill is needed to rise to power within one, I assure you.*" He'd laughed. It had been a shade more hollow a laugh than it might have been otherwise, but it had still been a laugh. "*I might assemble one for the sheer pleasure of forcing your hand. I suspect you would rule with an iron fist.*"

She had sniffed. She had not mentioned his brother again. "*You can try.*"

Tarek had a different way of trying. He'd pulled her astride him, pushing his way inside her again. Then he'd watched as she wriggled to accommodate him. It was his favorite show and no matter how many times he watched, it never grew old. Her indrawn breath, especially when she was already faintly swollen from before. The way she bit down on her lower lip. Her marvelous hips and how they moved against his as she adjusted to his length, his girth. The way she rocked slightly until it felt good.

And all the while she softened around him, drenching him with her fire.

Until there were no memories left to haunt him.

Until there was only Anya.

There was no way around it, he thought now, only half attending to the deeply boring world leaders standing around him. He was obsessed.

And he couldn't be any such thing. He was the King.

The country was the only obsession he allowed

himself. The only memories he permitted. How else could he have fought off Rafiq? How else would he rule?

Against his will, he found Anya in the crowd. He didn't know what he wanted. To assure himself he was not obsessed or to feed that obsession? But whatever dark thoughts he might have had in either direction, when he located her he was instantly struck by the way she was holding herself.

Anya was wearing a glorious gown in a Western style for this first celebration of the week. It was a sweeping number that left her collarbone bare, a perfect place for the jewels he'd placed there himself when he'd finished wringing them both dry earlier. The rest of the dress was a glorious fall to the floor in a deep aubergine shade that made her glow. Her glossy hair was swept up so the whole world might see the elegance of her neck, the delicate sweep of her jaw, and all of that was nothing next to the sophistication she seemed to carry in her bones.

She looked like a queen. His Queen.

But she was staring at the woman before her in a manner Tarek recognized all too well. Her shoulders were tight and her chin was tilted up at a belligerent angle that Tarek knew was a tell. It was outward evidence of her ferocity.

It should not have been happening at a party in her honor.

And certainly not in the presence of so many cameras. Though that particular consideration was an afterthought—another indication that Tarek was not in his right mind where this woman was concerned. Surely, with the international press present at this party, his only thoughts should have been on their joint performance instead of her feelings.

You are a king, he reminded himself icily. *Perhaps act like one.*

He excused himself and crossed to her, moving swiftly through the great hall. The crowd of guests parted before him as he moved, and he did not waste his time nodding greetings or allowing anyone to catch his eye. He bore down upon his betrothed.

And Anya alone did not instinctively move out of his way. She stayed where she was, only glancing his way—with a frown—when he appeared beside her.

"I do not care for the look on your face, *habibti*," Tarek told her. In his language, because the froth of a blonde woman before her and the older man beside her who looked as if he smelled something rank were clearly American.

Anya's gaze softened. Her frown smoothed out, and Tarek thought he saw something like relief there. He took his time shifting to gaze directly at the people who dared upset her. Here in the royal palace, right beneath his nose.

"Your Excellency," Anya murmured in formal greeting. She smiled at the couple. "Dad, Charisma, I would like to introduce you to Tarek bin Alzalam, the King of this country and my fiancé." Then she looked at him again. "Tarek, this is my father, Dr. Preston Turner, and his wife, Charisma Turner."

"Ah, yes." Tarek neither smiled nor offered his hand, as was his right as sovereign. That it also made the man before him *tut* in outrage was merely a bonus. "The doctor, yes?"

It was possible he made *doctor* sound a great deal like *snake*.

But then, Anya's father did not look sufficiently honored to find himself in the presence of a king. Nor particularly pleased to reunite with his only child after such a long separation—that had included said child's incarceration. Tarek did not expect or want an emotional display, certainly, but surely there should have been something other than the haughty expression on the older man's face.

"I was telling my daughter that I was forced to reschedule several surgeries," the man said, as if relaying an outrage. "In order to fly across the world at a moment's notice."

Then he waited, as if he expected Tarek to react to that.

And Tarek did. He gazed down at the man the way he imagined he might look at an insect, should it dare to begin buzzing at him. Right before he squashed it.

Beside him, Anya made a soft sound that he thought was a suppressed laugh.

"My father is referring to his schedule at the hospital," she said quickly. "He is…distressed that he had to alter it to come here for these celebrations. I explained to him that he could have come in later in the week, of course."

"You may not care what people think of you, Anya," her father said, making no apparent attempt to curtail the snide lash in his words. "But I'm afraid I do. However inconvenient it might be, I can hardly pretend this hasty wedding isn't happening. It's been all over the news."

"Your daughter is my choice of bride," Tarek said, without comprehension. "She is about to become the Queen of Alzalam, the toast of the kingdom. Yet you speak of your convenience?"

The man bristled in obvious affront. Tarek did not reply in kind, an example of his benevolence he suspected was lost on this small and unpleasant man.

"Rescheduling is such a nightmare," the blonde on his arm breathed, her eyes on her husband.

"Excuse us." Tarek's tone was dark as he took Anya's arm. "Let us leave you to contemplate your calendar. We will continue with the celebration."

He steered Anya away from her scowling father, doing his best not to scowl himself, as that would only cause general agitation in the crowds all around.

"I cannot comprehend the fact I found you discussing your father's *inconvenience*," he said in a low voice. "As if he was not standing in the ancient palace of Alzalam's kings, in the presence of a daughter who will become Queen. He should have been stretched out at your feet, begging your favor."

And would have been even a generation ago, but

the wider world tended to frown upon such things in these supposedly enlightened times.

Anya looked philosophical. Was Tarek the only one who could see the hurt beneath? And because he could see it, he could see nothing else.

"I suppose I should be grateful that no matter what he's doing, no matter where he finds himself or who he speaks to, my father is always…exactly the same," she said.

Tarek found himself even less philosophical as the night—and the week—wore on.

The kingdom overflowed with wedding guests and those who merely wished to use their King's wedding as an opportunity to celebrate, now that the troubles of the past year were well and truly over. There were celebrations in and out of the palace, all over the capital city and in the farthest villages alike, as the people celebrated not just Tarek and the bride he was taking, but this new era of the kingdom.

Tarek was deeply conscious of this. He had promised them a new world, a bright future, and this was the first happy bit of proof that he planned to deliver. And in a far different way than any of his ancestors would have. His brother was in jail, the insurgents had been fought back, and Tarek had no fear of the world's condemnation or attention—or he would not have been marrying this woman.

Now was a time for hope. His new Queen was the beacon of that hope.

Love grows in the most unlikely of places… the

more easily swayed papers sighed, from London to Sydney and back again.

From Convict to Queen! shouted the more salacious.

But either way, choosing this thoroughly American career woman—all previously considered epithets to his people—was having precisely the effect on Alzalam's image that Tarek had hoped it would. She was a success and their supposed love story even more so. All was going to plan, save his unfortunate obsession with the woman in question that he would far rather have coldly used as a pawn.

Yet no matter where he found himself in these endless parties, dinners, and the more traditional rituals prized by his people, and no matter the current state of his insatiable hunger for Anya herself, Tarek couldn't keep himself from noticing that Anya's father behaved more as if he was being tortured than welcomed into the royal, ruling family of an ancient kingdom.

"I told you," Anya said one night, looping her arms around his neck as he carried her from her terrace into her bedroom. He had not yet moved her things into the King's suite, in a gesture toward tradition—even if he did not intend to install her in the usual harem quarters. He wanted her much closer. "My father believes there is no greater more noble calling than his. What are kings and queens next to *the foremost neurosurgeon in all the land.*"

Tarek threw her on her bed and followed her

down. "He acts as if it is an insult that he is here at all."

Anya had sighed as if it didn't matter to her, yet Tarek was sure he'd seen a shadow move over her face. He hated it. "He has always been easily insulted. The real truth, I think, is that he's used to being the center of attention. That's really all there is to it."

"At his own daughter's wedding?"

"In fairness, if I was marrying almost anyone else he really would be the center of attention. Because the father of the bride commands a different part of the wedding where we come from. At the very least he would have stacked the guest list with his friends and associates, all of whom would be far more impressed with him than a collection of royals."

"Anya," Tarek had said, not exactly softly. "Why do you feel the need to treat this man with fairness when he feels no compunction to extend the same to you?"

She had looked stricken, then kissed him instead of answering.

Tarek understood that was an answer all its own.

Today there had been a gathering earlier for a wide swathe of guests, but the night featured a dinner for family only. Given the size of Tarek's immediate family, this meant a formal meal in one of the larger dining rooms, with all of Tarek's half siblings, their mothers, and their spouses invited to make merry. Compared to the other celebrations that had occurred this week, it was an intimate gathering. Tarek should have enjoyed introducing his bride to all his sisters and brothers—save the one, who no one dared mention.

But it was Anya's father who once again had Tarek's attention.

"It is a delight to welcome your daughter to the family," said Tarek's oldest half sister, Nur, smiling at the sour-faced doctor. Tarek wasn't surprised that his sister admired his choice of bride. Nur had not taken the princess route as many of their other half sisters had. She had a postdoctoral degree at Cambridge, she had married a highly ranked Alzalamian aristocrat who also happened to be a scientist, and she had never been remotely interested in or impressed by poor Nabeeha, at large in Canada. "A real doctor in the palace at last. I fear I am merely a doctor of philosophy, myself."

Anya smiled. "You're very kind."

Beside her, her father snorted.

That was objectionable enough. But Tarek found himself watching Anya. At the way she lowered her gaze and threaded her fingers together in her lap, as if she was trying to calm herself down. Or as if her father had not merely made himself look foolish, but had hurt her in some way.

Unacceptable, Tarek thought.

"I wouldn't call Anya a real doctor," her father said with a sniff. "There is such a thing as a waste of a medical degree. And for what? To wear pretty dresses and play Cinderella games? What a travesty."

Nur drew back, appalled. Anya's chin was set, her gaze still on her hands in her lap.

Tarek found he'd had enough.

"You forget yourself," he said softly from his place at the head of the table. Though he did not project his voice on the length of it, he knew that the rest of his family heard him.

A stillness fell over the room.

The doctor was staring at Tarek. "I beg your pardon?"

"It is denied," Tarek retorted. He leaned forward in his chair. "I do not know where it is you imagine you are, but let me enlighten you. This is the kingdom of Alzalam. *My* kingdom, which I have bled to defend." There was a chorus of cheers at that, startling the older man. "You are sitting at my table. The woman you insult will be my wife the day after tomorrow. Men have died for lesser insults."

There was more murmuring down the length of the table, rumbles of support from his family.

But Anya's father only blinked at him. "Anya would be the first to tell you that she hasn't quite lived up to expectations. She was raised to make a difference, not to…"

"Not to what?" Tarek asked.

Dangerously.

He shouldn't have been doing this, he knew. Not because there was any weakness in a man defending his woman—quite the opposite. A man who did not happily and thoroughly defend his woman, in Tarek's opinion, was no man at all. But because Anya would likely not thank him for complicating her family affairs.

But it was too late.

"Preston," said the man's wife, fluttering helplessly beside him. "You haven't even touched your food."

"Don't insert yourself into things you don't understand, Charisma," he replied in a cutting tone that made his wife—and daughter—flinch. "The adults are talking."

"Dad," Anya said then, in a fierce undertone. "This is not the time or the place."

"My daughter is a smart girl," the doctor said, glaring at Tarek. "I had high hopes that she might lead with her intellect. Make the right choices. But instead, this spectacle." He shook his head and looked at Anya. Pityingly, Tarek was astonished to note. "I told you what would happen if you joined that traveling aid organization. I even dared to hope that prison might get your head on straight for a change."

Anya shook her head at him. "You say that as if you were actually aware that I was in a dungeon all that time. I was under the impression you were maintaining plausible deniability so as not to make golf at the club too awkward."

"Of course I knew you were in prison, Anya," her

father snapped at her. "I can hardly avoid camera crews on my front lawn. What I don't understand is how you could come out of an experience like that and decide to make your life even less intelligible. What do you intend to do? Sit on a throne as you while your days away? Useless in every regard?"

Tarek did not like the way that Anya flushed at that, flashing a look at her stepmother. He remembered what she'd told him. That her stepmothers were allowed to be pretty and useless while she was meant to be smart. And it was clearly a downgrade to move from one column to the other.

"You will stop speaking, now," he decreed, and though the older man's eyes widened as if he planned to sputter out his indignation, he didn't make a sound. Like the coward he clearly was. "I will not bar you from your daughter's wedding, but one more word and I will have you deported."

Nur, sitting across from the Americans, did not applaud. Neither did her husband. But down the table, their other half siblings were not so circumspect.

"Tarek," Anya murmured. "Please."

Tarek kept his gaze trained on the man before him. The man who'd put shadows on his bride's face on what should have been a joyous occasion. More than once.

This was unforgivable as far as he was concerned.

"You and I know the truth, do we not?" Tarek did not look at Nur when she made a soft sound of agreement. Or at Anya, though he could sense her tension. "Your daughter is smart. Far smarter than you, evidently, which I imagine has scared you from the start. You wanted to control her, but you couldn't. And now look at you. A tiny little rooster of a man, prancing around a palace and acting as if it is his very own barnyard. It is not. I am a king. You are a doctor whose worth lies only in the steadiness of his hands. And your daughter has saved countless lives and will now save more in a different role, because that is real power. Not ego—"

The older man opened his mouth.

Tarek lifted a brow. "I do not make idle threats."

He waited as Anya's father turned an alarming shade of red. Tarek shot a look at Nur, who started up the conversation anew, and then Tarek sat back and stopped paying the older man the attention he did not deserve.

And it was only when the room filled with warmth and laughter again that Anya looked over at him and smiled.

Then mouthed her thanks.

Tarek had received gratitude before in the form of treaties. Surrenders. Invaluable gifts too innumerable to name, many of which were displayed with pride in this very palace.

But Anya's simple *thank you* lodged inside him like a heartbeat.

Until his chest felt filled with it—with her. Until it threatened to take his breath.

Until he wondered what he was going to do with this.

How was he going handle this woman he needed to be his Queen when she made him *feel*?

And not like the King he was—but like the regular man he could not permit himself to become.

Because Tarek knew well the cost of forgetting himself.

Rafiq had been the only person alive Tarek had felt he could truly be himself with. They had been so close. Tarek had depended on him. And Rafiq had used that affection to stab Tarek in the back.

Literally.

"*You cannot permit yourself the failings and petty feelings of common men*," his mother had told him time and time again. "*In a king these are fatal flaws, Tarek. Remember that.*"

He remembered her words too well.

What was he going to *do*?

CHAPTER NINE

THE DAY OF the wedding dawned at last.

Anya had been waiting for the sun to rise for hours, unable to sleep.

She had been ceremoniously escorted to her bedchamber the night before by Tarek's sisters and aunts. It was tradition for the groom's relatives to guard the bride and so they had, though the royal family's version of "guarding" had included more laughter and abundant food. They had told Anya involved tales about Tarek as a child, omitting any mention of his treacherous brother. They had painted her pictures of what he'd been like as an adolescent, too aware of the weight he would one day carry.

All with a kind of easy, warm familiarity that Anya had never experienced before. She hardly knew what to call it.

It wasn't until she'd gone and stretched out in her bed with only the moon for company that she realized it was…family. They were a family. More, they acted the way she had always imagined a family should. Teasing, laughing. Gestures of quiet support when more serious topics were addressed. The very fact they'd all gathered together to celebrate Anya when all they really knew about her was that she was Tarek's choice of bride.

But they loved him, so that was all they needed.

Anya had stared out at the moon and accepted a hard truth. She had long told herself that she didn't need the connections that other people took for granted. She had her chilly father, she'd told people when the subject came up, and that was more than enough family for her, thank you. She had friends, though she didn't see them often enough.

But Tarek's family wasn't the Turner version of family. It was the version she realized now that she'd always imagined in her head—but had assured herself didn't exist.

It left her something like shaken to discover that she was wrong.

More, it made her miss Tarek.

The solid weight of his stare. The sheer perfection of his body and the things he could do with it. The fire that burned so bright between them that she found she didn't want to live without it, not even for a night.

She suspected she knew what words she could use to describe all the things she felt about the man she was marrying, and none of them were *practical*. None of them were appropriate press releases.

But they were right there on her tongue. Dangerously close to spilling out at the slightest provocation.

"*Until tomorrow,*" Tarek had murmured much earlier that night, out in the desert where they had taken part in rituals he told her his people had considered holy since the earth was young.

It had felt more than holy to Anya.

The sand and the sky. The stars.

The two of them in a circle of fire while the elders sang over them.

Anya sighed now, remembering the stark beauty all around them. The press of the songs and chants against her skin, winding all around their clasped hands.

"*If I hadn't ended up in your prison, I never would have known,*" she'd whispered to Tarek. "*How much beauty there is in the world. Particularly here.*"

Particularly you, she'd thought, perilously close to letting those words she shouldn't say spill out to join the rest of the night's magic.

"*Tomorrow, habibti,*" he'd said, his dark eyes gleaming.

Out on her favorite chaise, Anya waited as the sun rose. The city below her shook itself to life in preparation. Songs filled the air, alive with the sweetness of the coming day. She pulled her throw tighter around her, breathing in the desert air mixed with the palace's usual *bakhoor*, a smoky scent that would always be Tarek to her. She sighed as the first tendrils of light and color snuck across the sky while she watched. Yellows and oranges. A glorious purple.

As the sun climbed, the air warmed.

Anya did, too.

And the light danced all over her, reminding her that she was still free. That stone cells were a thing of the past. That what lay before her might not look like anything she'd thought she wanted—or should want—but made her feel, finally, that it might actually be possible to be happy.

A revolution, she thought.

Only then did she get up and head inside to begin the long process of getting ready for her wedding. Her royal wedding that would be broadcast around the world as part of the press release portion of the bargain she'd made with Tarek.

And in Alzalam, wedding preparations were a largely public affair. Her seamstresses swept in and out. All of Tarek's family returned, flooding in as if the dressing of the bride was a party they were throwing—more for themselves than her.

Once Anya was dressed in her finery and several thousand photographs had been taken, men were allowed in as well. Trays of food were brought in while the guests mingled all throughout the sprawling suite. Anya stood in one of the smaller salons, catching glimpses of herself in the enormous mirror propped against the wall while she thanked the guests for coming, one after the next, until it was all little more than a blur.

She looked like something out of a dream she hadn't known she'd had. Her dressmakers had truly outdone themselves, somehow managing to fuse both Tarek's world and hers into the sweep of the long white gown. She looked exactly as she should—like a beacon of a kind of hope.

Like the future she imagined here, bright beyond measure.

And then, perhaps inevitably, her father walked in.

She could tell by the way he marched into the salon, holding his body sharply and crisply, that he was still in high dudgeon from the other night. That he was *deeply offended* hung around him like a cloud, likely discernible even to those who hadn't spent a lifetime parsing his moods. The way he snapped the door shut behind him only underscored it.

That he wanted her to apologize to him—even though he'd had an entire day to get over what had happened at that dinner, having not been part of yesterday's rituals—was clear by the imperious way he glared at her as he stood there, Charisma standing to one side and slightly behind him, as if he didn't notice his only daughter on a dais before him.

In a bridal gown, with jewels in her hair.

Tarek's sister Nur had teared up when she'd seen Anya. "*You look like everything my brother deserves*," she'd said.

But her own father looked at her and saw only himself.

Anya kept herself from sighing, barely, because that wasn't anything new, was it?

"It's so nice of you to come and wish me health and happiness, Dad," she said, and she imagined she saw Charisma wince a bit. "Thank you."

Dr. Preston Turner did not wince. He hardly reacted.

"This is a low, even for you," he told her, the force of his outrage making his voice even crisper and more precise than usual. "It's not enough that you should humiliate yourself in this way and on such a grand scale when you are clearly in no fit state to make decisions of this magnitude. Look at the mess you've already made of your life. But that you should sit silently by and allow me to suffer such attacks…"

His voice trailed off. Anya mused, almost idly, that she had never seen her father at a loss for words in all her life. Not until now.

Point to Tarek, she couldn't help but think.

Sadly, he recovered. With a furious glare. "I thought I couldn't be more disappointed in you, Anya. Trust you to go ahead and prove me wrong yet again."

Anya looked at this man who she had tried and failed to please for her entire life. This man whose expectations sat so heavily upon her that she had found a dungeon preferable to the weight of them.

She knew she favored her mother in looks, but she had always imagined that there were similarities between her and her father anyway. Not his famous hands, maybe. Not his drive. But certain expressions. The color of their eyes.

But today she looked at him and saw a stranger.

No, she corrected herself. *Not quite a stranger. Something worse than that.*

A father who had made himself a stranger to his only child. By choice.

"Your disappointment has nothing to do with me," she said, with a quiet force she knew her father did not miss. "I can't help you with it or save you from it."

Out of the corner of her eye, she could see her stepmother, fluttering as ever as she murmured something to Preston.

"For God's sake," her father snapped at her. "Just stand still, Charisma."

"She's not your lapdog, Dad." Anya shook her head at him. "I know you like to think she's stupid, but she's not. She knows exactly how to handle you, which is an art I certainly failed to master. You're lucky to have her."

"I'll thank you to keep your opinions about my marriage to yourself," her father barked.

Though next to him, Charisma blinked. Then smiled.

Anya smoothed her hands over the front of her dress, because it made her think of her wedding and the life she would live here, far away from her father's toxic disappointment. "I thought we were commenting on marriages today. Isn't that what you came to do? Tell me your opinions about the man I'm marrying in a few hours? Or did you miss that I'm standing here in a bridal gown?"

"I would advise you not to speak to me in such a disrespectful manner, Anya."

"Or what?" It was a genuine question. "I'm not a small child you can spank. Or one of your surgical residents or nurses you can bully. You're standing in a palace that is to be my home, in a kingdom I am to be Queen of in a few hours. Really, Dad. What do you plan to do to me if I don't obey you?"

"I'm your father," Preston thundered at her.

"And I'm your daughter." Anya felt the swell of something inside her, bigger than a wave. It crashed over her, into her, and she couldn't tell if it was drowning her or drawing her out to sea. But she found she didn't have it in her to care. "I'm your daughter and you treat me a lot worse than a lapdog. I've spent my whole life trying to make you proud of me, but I realize now that it's impossible. No one can make you happy, Dad. No one. You don't have it in you. And that has to do with you, not me. I can't make you a different man. What I can do is stop pretending that I'm someone I'm not when you don't even appreciate the effort."

She had been afraid of saying something like that her whole life. And now she had, and she didn't feel a burst of freedom and joy, the way she'd thought she would. Instead, she found she felt sad. Not for herself, but for him. For the relationship they'd never had.

"I have no idea what you mean," he was raging at her. "You had every opportunity to do the right thing and you squandered it, each and every time. That's on you, Anya."

And Anya was already swimming far from land. This was already happening. Last night there had been too many stars to count, and here was her father, determined to ruin it.

She lifted her hands, then dropped them. Not a surrender, because it felt too…right.

Too long overdue.

"I don't want to be a doctor," she told him, the words she'd never dared say out loud falling from her lips as if it had always been easy to say them. As if she should have long ago. Because there was no sadness in this. There was only truth. "I never did."

Charisma actually gasped.

"Don't be ridiculous," her father snapped. "You have obviously let this awful place get to you. You need help, Anya. Psychological help. You've always been far too emotional and your ordeal has clearly put you over the edge."

What struck her then wasn't the dismissive tone her father used. Anya was used to that. It wasn't the contemptuous look on his face, because, of course, she was familiar with that, too.

But she wasn't the same woman she'd been the night she'd gotten arrested. Those eight months had changed her.

Yet she still paused for a moment, tried to look

inside herself, to see if anything that he said had merit. After all, hadn't she wondered if she was suffering from some kind of psychiatric issue? Hadn't she made little jokes to herself—and her friends once she'd started using her mobile again—about Stockholm syndrome?

No, came a voice from inside her, deep and certain and undeniably her own. *That's your father talking. You know what you feel. You always have.*

"It doesn't matter what I want to do with my life," she said quietly. "In the end, it's really very simple. You either love me, Dad—or you don't."

And then she waited. She didn't look past him to the closed door with the palace staff waiting on the other side. Guests and soon-to-be in-laws celebrating as her own father couldn't. She didn't look at her stepmother, who was still standing at Preston's side. She didn't fidget. She didn't look away.

Anya trained her gaze on her father, direct and open. And watched as something impatient moved over his face. With possibly more than a little distaste, mixed right in.

"My God, Anya," he said. And when he spoke, that distaste was unmistakable. He didn't quite recoil, but managed to give the impression that he might at any moment. "You've become completely unglued." His gaze, so much like her own, sharpened in a way she hoped hers never had. She found she was bracing herself, though she couldn't have said why when she knew him. There was no point bracing for the inevitable, was there? "Unglued, emotional, and pitiful. Just like your mother."

He meant it like a bomb, and it exploded inside her like a blinding flash of light. She stared back at him, seeing nothing but his gaze like a machete, aimed right at her.

Aimed to hurt. To leave wounds.

On some level, Anya was aware that her father, brimming with triumph at the blow he'd landed, had turned and was marching for the door. She met her stepmother's gaze, bright blue and stricken, but all either one of them could do was stare. Then Charisma, too, scurried for the exit.

And once the door was open, the room filled up again. There was laughter again, sunlight and brightness and that glorious sense of expectation and hope that Anya herself had felt so keenly earlier.

She was aware of all of it. She smiled for her photographs. She shook hands, smiled wider, and did her job as the Queen she would shortly become.

Yet all the while, the bomb her father had lobbed at her kept blowing up inside her. Over and over again.

But not, she thought, in the way he'd intended it to.

Because all she could seem to concentrate on were memories of her mother she'd have sworn she didn't have.

She'd been seven when her mother died. Anya wasn't one of those who had memories dating back to the cradle, but she did have memories. That was the point. When all this time she'd convinced herself she didn't.

"*You are brave, Anya,*" her mother had used to whisper to her. She would gather Anya in her lap, tucked away in the corner of the house that was only theirs. Sometimes she would read books. Other times, she would have Anya tell stories about her day. About school, her friends, her teachers. Or perhaps her stuffed animals, if that was a mood Anya was in. "*You are brave and you are fierce. You can do anything you want to do, do you hear me?*"

"*I hear you, Mama,*" Anya would reply.

What she remembered now was that when she'd thought of all the things she could do, it had never been becoming a doctor. She had been far more interested in learning how to fly, with or without wings, much less a plane. And dancing, which she had loved more than anything back then, despite her distinct lack of talent or ability. And the masterpieces she'd created with her crayons, that she'd secretly believed were the sort of thing she ought to do forever, if only as a gift to the world.

Anya remembered walking in the backyard holding tight to her mother's hand, listening intently as Mama had pointed out a bird here, a bug there. She had repeated the names of flowers and plants, all the trees that towered over them, then made up stories to explain the tracks in the dirt.

She remembered her mother's laugh, her joyful smile, and if she focused as hard as she could, she was convinced that she could almost remember the particular smell of her mother's skin, right in the crook of her neck where Anya liked to rest her face when she was sleepy. Or sick.

Or just because.

Once one memory returned to her, all the rest followed suit. She was flooded with them. And it was clear to her, when it was finally time and she was led from her rooms, that somehow, this was her mother's way of being here today.

It was what her private moment with her father should have been, yet wasn't. All these memories dressed up more brightly now, and almost better for having been lost to her for so many years.

Because it felt like her mother was here. Right here. With her she walked through the palace halls, surrounded by Tarek's sisters and aunts. It was as if her mother was holding fast to her hand all over again, her simple presence making Anya feel safe. Happy.

And absolutely certain that there was nothing wrong with her. No psychological damage from her time in jail. Just hope.

Anya knew, then, that every step she took was right and good, and better still, her mother was beside her for all of it.

She waited outside the great ballroom, open today to the even grander courtyard beyond, and she knew something else, too. As surely and as fully as if the words were printed deep into her own flesh. As if they were scars like Tarek's, angry and red at first, then fading into silver with the passage of time.

But scars all the same.

Because her heart was pounding at her. Her stomach was fluttery. But she knew that none of that was panic.

She thought of her long-lost mother and the things she'd said so long ago. That Anya was brave and fierce, capable of choosing any life she wanted. Anya had believed her.

Anya believed her so hard, so completely, that when she was gone it was as if she'd taken all of that with her.

Without her, Anya had never felt brave. Or anything like fierce. And she hadn't known what she wanted, except her mother back.

But that was never on offer.

And without her mother there, there was nothing to temper her father's coldness. Back then, he'd been a different man. She could remember him, too. Never as warm as her mother had been, but he'd smiled then. He'd laughed. He'd danced with her mother in the backyard on warm summer nights, and held Anya between them, her bare feet on his shoes. In every way that mattered, she'd lost both her parents when her mother died.

Anya almost felt sympathy for him, in retrospect. But back then, as a little girl awash in grief, all she'd known was that she didn't want to cause her father more pain. She'd wanted him to love her.

She'd wanted him to gather her up in his lap, tell her stories, and make her feel better. Dance with her in the yard while the summer night stretched out above them, warm and soft. But he didn't.

He never did.

So she'd made herself cold instead, to please him.

But she was not cold, no matter how hard she tried. And maybe, Anya thought, as she waited for a panic attack to hit her when surely it should— poised to walk down an aisle to marry a king in the full view of the better part of the planet—the panic attacks had been her actual, real feelings trying to get out all along.

The doors opened before her, then. And then it was happening.

She was walking toward Tarek. She could see him there, waiting for her at the end of the aisle, magnificent in every way.

But best of all, looking straight at her. Into her.

As if this thing between them was fate and they'd been meant for each other all along.

When she finally reached him, he took her hands and they began to speak old words. Ancient vows. Sharing who they were and becoming something else.

Husband and wife. King and Queen.

And so much more.

But inside, Anya made a different vow, there before the assembled throng. That she would not be cold another day in her life. That she would never again be buried in stone or locked away behind iron. That she would not allow herself to feel dead while she was alive.

Not with him. Not with this man who had freed her from a cell first, and then from the life she'd never really wanted.

So she married him, and then she lived.

She danced at the reception. She smiled until her cheeks hurt. And when Tarek finally stole her away, bundling her into a helicopter that raced across the desert, suspended between the shifting, undulating sands beneath and the heavens above, she loved him so much that she thought it might burst out of her like a comet. Another bomb, and a better one this time.

Anya didn't know how she kept it inside.

The helicopter dropped them in an oasis straight out of a fairy tale. The water in the many pools was an indigo silk, lapping gently against the sand as the breeze hit it. Palm trees rustled all around, while waterfalls tumbled over rocks like a song.

And a glorious, sprawling tent blazed with welcoming light, beckoning them in.

"Welcome, my Queen," Tarek said when the helicopter rose back into the air and the sound of its rotors faded away. He had led her into the vast living area of the tent, outfitted with a thousand pillows and low tables, like a desert fantasy. Now he smiled down at her. "This is the royal oasis. Some claim the water is sacred. Some believe it heals. We will have to test it, you and I."

Anya was sure that all the things she felt must be emblazoned on her face. But that wasn't enough. Nothing could be *enough*.

She reached up, placed her palms on either side of his beautiful face, and sighed a little as his strong arms came around her. She thought, *this is home*.

She was finally home.

"Tarek," she breathed, with her whole heart. With everything she had and everything she was. With all the bright hope inside her after this magical, beautiful day. "I love you."

And watched as his face turned to stone.

CHAPTER TEN

"YOU MUST BE TIRED," Tarek said, taking each of Anya's hands in his. He pulled them away from his face, as if that would erase the words she'd said.

The words that seemed to fill the tent and more, roll out over the desert like a storm, blanketing everything.

Burying him alive.

"Not particularly," she replied, that frown he liked too much appearing between her brows. "On the contrary, I've never felt more alive. And in love, Tarek."

In case he'd missed that the first time.

And there was that pressure in his chest. That pounding thing inside him that he thought was his heart, but it seemed too large. Too dangerous.

Too catastrophic.

"Come now, Doctor," he said, not sure he sounded like himself—but it was hard to know what it was he heard with that storm in him. "There are far more pleasurable things to do tonight than forget ourselves."

She was dressed in that gown that he had spent

long hours today imagining taking off her, one centimeter at a time. Her hair was set with precious jewels, each representing a different facet of the kingdom. She was a vision, she was now his Queen, and the last thing in the world he wanted to talk about was love.

But Anya did not melt into him. She did not shake off the gathering storm. Instead, her hands found her hips.

"Forget ourselves?" she echoed.

This oasis was one of Tarek's favorite places in all the world, and yet he never came here enough. It had been years. There always seemed far too many things he needed to do in the city, far too many responsibilities in the palace alone. He had looked forward to the time he would spend here with Anya more than he should have.

It was his own fault. He accepted that. He'd allowed his obsession with her to get the better of him.

No wonder it had come to this.

"I take responsibility," he told her, as he had the day they'd met. When she had sat opposite him in her prison grays in a roomful of dizzy light.

When he had found himself stunned, the way he had been ever since.

His declaration did not have the effect on her that he'd been hoping it would. It was hard to say it had any effect at all. Anya only continued to stare up at him, still frowning, her hands still propped on her hips.

"I'm beginning to think that you say that as a way

to deflect attention. It's nice that you want to take responsibility, Tarek. But no responsibility needs to be taken." She lifted her shoulders, then dropped them, a parody of a careless shrug when he could see the stubborn angle of her chin. "I'm in love with you."

"We are married," he ground out. "There is no need for…this."

"We can pretend that I married you because I was suddenly seized with the need for a throne." She actually rolled her eyes, something he would have taken exception to under any other circumstances. "But I think you and I both know that there are a great many more convenient ways to stop practicing medicine. I could have simply…stopped. People do that. Who knows? I could have moved to a quiet little town and opened a charming bookshop, if I liked. There are a thousand better solutions to a career that makes me unhappy than marrying a sheikh. A king. And everything that goes with that."

"We discussed what this marriage is and isn't," he managed to say, aware that his voice was little better than a growl. "Romantic fantasies were never a part of this."

"Oh, right." Another eye roll, that Tarek liked no better than the first. "I should have realized. This is the part where you attempt to convince me that I don't know my own feelings. This is where you tell me that I've somehow confused love with something else. A bit too much of the bubbly stuff, perhaps? I can see how a person might mistake the two."

"I think," Tarek said, carefully, though he was not doing a good job at keeping that seething, furious note out of his voice, "that it is easy to let the pageant of a wedding…become confusing."

Anya aimed that smirk of hers at him. "Are you confused?"

"I warned you, did I not?" And he was less careful, then. The storm was too intense, too rough and wild. "You can't help yourself. You're culturally predisposed to romanticize everything."

Any other woman of his acquaintance would have backed down in a hurry, but this was Anya.

"I wasn't sitting in my jail cell, rhapsodizing about the possibility of being swept off into the arms of a desert king, thank you very much," she hurled at him. "If I fantasized about you at all back then, it was to imagine your comeuppance. And I don't think that I've romanticized what happened since. We had an agreement, sure. But we also had everything else."

Tarek wanted to touch her. And knew that if he did, it would be betraying everything he stood for. Everything he was.

And still he had to draw his hands back as they moved toward her, seemingly of their own accord.

"I do not believe in love." He said it with brutal finality, but he felt no joy in it when she flinched. "I should have made that clear from the start. I rather thought I did. Love has no place in an arrangement like this. How could it? I am a king, Anya."

"You are," she agreed. She shook her head as if

she didn't understand. Or as if she didn't think *he* understood. "But you're also a man. And that man—"

"There is no difference between the two," he said gruffly. "Don't flatter yourself, Anya. I married you because it was convenient. Marrying a Western woman, a doctor who the world decided was a prisoner of conscience, was a calculated political move. It suggests things about me that I would like the world to believe. That I am progressive. That I am capable of softer feelings and fairy tales. That my regime and my kingdom are soft and cuddly in some way, or that I have a more accessible side. When none of those things are true."

Her hands had moved from her hips and were hanging on her sides, curled into fists now. Another gesture of disrespect he would accept from no one else in his presence. She'd gone pale, but she was still holding his gaze, no matter that her eyes were far brighter than before.

What she did not do was back down.

"I understand the nature of a press release," she said, from between her teeth. "But that's not the only thing that's between us."

Tarek roamed away from her then. The tent was expansive, this room in particular, but it was still only a tent. There was only so much distance he could put between them.

He heard her follow him, her dress rustling in a way that set fire to parts of his imagination he wished he could cut out. Or dig out with his own fingers, whatever worked, just to be...*himself* again.

This was not how he had imagined this evening going.

When Tarek had looked up and seen her—there at the other end of the aisle that his staff had made through the center of the crowd, laden with flower petals to mark her way—he'd worried that he might truly have died where he stood.

Right there, in full view of the world.

He felt as if the skies had opened up and rain had poured down on this stretch of ancient desert that was lucky to see water from above perhaps twice in a decade. More, he was sure he'd been struck by lightning.

Repeatedly.

If possible, she was even more beautiful than she'd been only the night before, when he'd been bound to her in the desert, the fires all around them flickering over her and making her glow.

Tarek had wondered how it could be that every time he looked at her it was as if he'd never seen her before. He felt that stunning jolt of recognition. His heart beat at him, hard. He felt the punch of it in his gut. And always, that heavy fire in his sex that was only hers.

It was not Alzalamian tradition for a father to walk a bride to her husband. It was rare that a bride's family had even been present in weddings of old, when brides had been used to end wars and make allies of enemies. Tarek had never been gladder that he was made of this place, these sands and these proud tribes, because even the sight of her dour father would have marred the perfection he'd seen moving toward him on her own.

A vision in white. Petals at her feet and glittering jewels in her hair.

His Queen. His woman. His Anya.

Her gaze was fixed on him as if he was the sun. She was smiling, brighter than the desert sky far above them in the grand courtyard.

There was a part of him that knew news organizations from around the world, set up around the courtyard with their cameras, would capture that smile. That it would sell their story better than anything else could. Tarek was aware of it the way he was aware of the sky, the heat, the crowd. All the inevitabilities, but he didn't care about it the way he should have. He didn't feel as if it was a job well done, that smile of hers, or as if he ought to sit around patting himself on the back for the show.

All he could think was that her smile was his.

His.

For the first time in as long as he could remember, possibly ever, Tarek had resented the fact that he was the King. That he could not enjoy Anya's joyful smile privately. That he could not keep this perfect, exquisite vision of his Anya walking toward him to marry him to himself.

I do not wish to share her, he had thought.

And when she finally reached him, he'd gazed down at her in a kind of shock, torn between what he wanted and what was.

Duty and desire, as always.

But there was only one winner in that fight, and ever had been.

Tarek knew that. He had always known that. And yet here he stood, engaged in futile battles inside himself while she looked at him with eyes so soft it made him ache, speaking of *love*.

"You can't really mean to tell me that you think there isn't more between us than a bargain we made," Anya said from behind him.

He turned and braced himself, but she didn't look the way he expected her to look. Her arms were folded and she was glaring at him. She was not cringing. She was certainly not frail and fainting. If she was awash in whatever emotions he'd seen in her eyes outside, he could see no trace of it on her.

This is your American doctor, he reminded himself. *In case you have forgotten.*

Not the sweetly pliant woman who smiled at him like he was a sunrise and ran all over him like the heat of the day.

"You're talking about sex," he said, harshly. "I won't pretend I don't enjoy it. But it is only sex."

Tarek meant that to hurt. To cut her in half, or at least stop this conversation. And he did not admire that he had that in him. That urge to cause pain that did not speak well of him or his ability to control himself no matter the situation. How had he imagined he'd been tested before? He clearly had not been.

But he didn't take those words back, either.

He should have known better. This was Anya.

She laughed.

And by the time she stopped, he found his teeth were gritted. His jaw clenched so hard he was surprised he didn't hear something break.

"Oh, Tarek." There was still laughter in her voice, and she shook her head a little as she said his name. "You can't really think that I'll suddenly and magically believe that what happened between us is *just sex*, because you say so. It doesn't work that way."

"You are mistaken," he said, though his mouth was full of glass, he was sure of it.

"I was there." It was as if she hadn't heard him speak. Her gaze never wavered. "I know better."

And something inside him was shaking. Shaking, crumbling, turning to ash and that bitter glass even as he stood there. Suggesting that what he'd taken to be the solid iron foundation of who he was, who he needed to be, had only ever been wishful thinking after all.

"I understand what it is you want," he told her, trying to sound less like broken pieces and more like a king. "But you cannot have it. Royal marriages have always been thus. Each one of us has very specific duties, Anya. I must rule the kingdom. You must support the throne. There will be heirs and they must be raised to respect the country, its people, the traditions that make us who we are, and the future we must make happen if we are to thrive."

"That sounds like a civics lesson," she threw at him. "I'm talking about our marriage."

"Our marriage has even more rules," he retorted. "How could you think otherwise? This is not one of your romances. This is a union that must produce the next King. You and I do not belong to each other, Anya. We are not lovers. I belong to the kingdom. And you must know your place."

"My place." Her eyes glittered with temper and something else Tarek didn't think he wished to define. "Maybe you'd better tell me exactly what you think that is."

"I have been telling you." His voice was an iron bar and he wished he still was, deep within. He wished she hadn't made him doubt he ever could be again. "What do you imagine this last month has been?"

She did not laugh at that, as he half expected she would, this woman who sobbed out her pleasure as if she might never recover and then faced him down as no man alive would dare. He saw something in that gaze of hers falter as she searched his face. He told himself he did not wish to know what she looked for. "This last month?"

"Yes, Anya." He started toward her then, the lanterns flickering all around them. The tent was lush, done up in deep colors, soft rugs, and everything that might make the cold of a desert night more comfortable. But it might as well have been a stark, empty cell for all he noticed. "What did you think? I have been teaching you how to be the Queen I want."

"I didn't realize that class was in session." There was that brightness in her eyes again, but she didn't give in to it. She stood taller, lifted her chin the way he thought she always would, and as ever with this woman, met his gaze.

Defiantly, he thought.

But Tarek was an expert at putting down rebellions. And he knew that if he did not stop this one before it started, it would sweep them both up. He had seen it happen.

He had spent his childhood surrounded by his father's wives. Some of them loved his father. Others loved his power. But love was always at the heart of the jealous wars that swept through the harem, pitting wife against wife and even half siblings against each other sometimes. All for love.

Practical wives, like his mother, kept themselves above the fray.

"A queen in love with the King is but a silly woman in love with an inconstant man," his mother had told him long ago, in the dialect that marked her as a member of the fiercest of all the Alzalam tribes. He knew his father had been forced to fight for her—literally, in a bare-fisted battle against her eldest brother. Only when he won did his mother's people, and his mother, consider his proposal. *"The world is filled with such women in love with lesser men. But*

*there is only one King of Alzalam. And I choose to
be his Queen first, last, and always.*"

He had to make Anya see.

"I have taught you well," he said as he drew close,
impressed as ever that she did not back down. Even
when he stood over her, perfectly placed to put his
hands on her in temper. In passion. In any way he
liked, but she looked unmoved by his proximity. "I
taught you the kinds of meals that I prefer and how
I like to eat them. I taught you how to give me your
surrender when I wish it. Each and every kind of
release I prefer. And how to please me with your
compliance."

She shook her head. "Silly me. I thought *I* taught
you that there's nothing wrong with taking out your
frustrations on a willing participant."

"There's nothing I don't like about you, Doctor,"
Tarek gritted out, because that was no more than the
truth. "I like your sharp tongue. I like your temper
and your brain. And I think you know I like the plea-
sures of your flesh. But you must never mistake the
matter. Those are part of the bargain we have made.
Love does not enter into it."

"I think," she said softly, her eyes glittering, "that
His Majesty protests too much."

"There it is again. That maudlin belief that all
things end up tied in a bow while something sen-
timental plays in the distance. I understand that
you can't help it. You can't change where you came

from." He sighed. "But it's not real, Anya. It will never be real."

"I don't believe you."

"You don't have to believe me. It makes no difference. Not believing me won't make what I'm telling you any less true or real. It will only cause you heartache. Facts are facts whether you choose to believe them, or do not."

"Tarek," she began, a kind of storm in her eyes. "You must know that I can see—"

But he did not wish to know what she saw. He *could not* know what she saw.

He had only let his guard down once, and he bore the scars of that mistake.

He refused to do it again.

"Very well then," he bit off, wrapping his hands around her upper arms and jerking her toward him, as he should have done from the start. "Let me show you."

And he set his mouth to hers in a punishing kiss.

But as sensation stormed through him, lighting him up and making him yearn for things he knew better than to want, Tarek suspected that the real punishment was his, not hers.

CHAPTER ELEVEN

HIS KISS WAS ELECTRIC.

Anya could feel it in every single inch of her body, tearing her up. Making her wonder how a person could function when they were nothing but pieces, scattered and torn and tossed to the wind. Burned alive, yet wanting nothing more than to keep burning.

She had half a mind to pull away. Slap him, maybe, not that she wanted to cause him pain. But she wanted to *wake him up*.

To prove to him that he was wrong about this and she was right.

That not only did she love him, but he loved her, too.

But Tarek was kissing her, and it didn't take much for her to forget that there was anything in the world but that.

All the things she'd been thinking all day seemed to course through her then, its own kind of power source. Until everything was something far hotter and brighter than electricity, and she could feel it inside her, twisting all around and then sinking down deep.

To where she would always run hot and soft for him. All for him.

"This is what we are," he gritted out, in her ear. "This is what I want from you."

She wanted to protest. She wanted to beat him away with her fists. Or her mind did, anyway.

Because her body wanted nothing more than to be close to him. To be devoured by him and to devour him in turn. To be wrapped around him, and then, gloriously, lifted up into his arms once more.

Where I belong, she couldn't help but think.

No matter how many times he tried to tell her otherwise.

He carried her through the tent, one section after the next. She had the impression of salons made of tapestries, delicately carved furnishing, and wide wooden trunks. But she only knew they'd reached a bedroom when he laid her down on a wide, soft bed. Lanterns lit up the brightly patterned walls and made their own shapes out of shadows.

But all Anya could really focus on was Tarek.

His robes were ivory and gold again, but there was far more gold tonight. The light caught at it, making him gleam. He was resplendent and beautiful, powerful and pitiless, and she loved him so much and so hard it made her feel lightheaded.

That in no way made her *less* mad at him.

Anya was panting as much from the force of the

things she wanted to say to him as his deep, drugging kisses, and she pushed herself up on her elbows so she could glare at him with the full force of her displeasure.

But all he did was follow her down to the bed, making them both groan as their bodies came together. He wasted no time in getting his hands on her, up beneath skirts and then streaking up to her knees. He found her upper thighs, and took a moment to trace the place where her stockings were attached with clips. Then he moved on, finding the white-hot, molten truth of her. Of this.

Of them.

Tarek stroked her then, intent and deep. She fell back down into the soft embrace of bed, piled high with silk and linen and surrounded by the scent that rolled over her the way this man—her *husband*, her King—did. She told herself to fight, but she was unable to do anything at all but lift her hips to take his clever fingers as they found their way into her slick, wet heat.

And she knew that she should be ashamed of this. That he could tell her there was nothing between them but sex, then prove it so easily. That she could claim she loved him and sex was the least of it, then succumb to his touch so wantonly.

But her hips lifted with abandon. Her back arched to give him better access. She was moaning out his name, even before he began to thrust his fingers deep inside her.

His other hand moved to her face, guiding her mouth to his all over again. Taking what he wanted. Showing her who she was.

Tarek kissed her, deep and hot, dark and demanding.

And when she broke apart, it was against his mouth. He groaned back as if he was consuming every last noise she made. As if she was his, and the sounds she made were his, and he was branding her mouth and sex alike.

But it was not love, he would claim. It was only sex, this mad possession.

Tarek moved over her and she could feel his hands working between them. A tug here, and adjustment there. Then the broad head of his hardness found her slick folds.

He waited.

Anya opened her eyes to meet his, stark and commanding.

"I love you," she whispered.

Tarek made a rough noise, then he was thrusting inside her, deep and hard. Reward or punishment, or both wrapped in the same shock of connection and belonging, hunger and dark delight—it was hard to tell.

She'd had him so many times by now. She knew his body so well. She knew his scent, his weight, the glory he could work with a twist of his hips or that merciless mouth of his.

She knew too much.

And this was different from what had come before. This was a storm all its own, a wildly different claiming.

It was raw, untamed, and just this side of *too much*.

It was like a fever. It was all those things she'd felt all day, whirling around and around, all of them a crisis.

And still he pounded into her, braced there above her, as he made her his in a new way to suit the new things they were to each other.

Husband and wife. King and Queen.

This.

He could call it what he liked. Anya knew better.

But still, when the explosion came rushing at her, she wasn't entirely sure she would survive it. Or even if she wished to.

Tarek let her fall apart first, but he kept going until she sobbed. His name, maybe. Or a cry for the mercy she both did and didn't want. Until her fingers dug so hard into the back of the robes he still wore that she felt a nail break.

Still he continued.

Proving a point, she was sure. Driving them both wild. Making her shake and shake, sensations roaring through her with such intensity it almost scared her.

"I love you," she cried out as she hurtled off a cliff she hadn't seen coming.

And only then did Tarek follow, with a roar she

felt shake through her all over again, like a new kind of shattering.

And there was no drifting off into bliss. There was no oblivion.

Tarek lifted his head, shifting his weight to his elbows. Anya was too aware of how he was covering her then, that rangy body of his, heavy and muscled everywhere, pressing her down into the bed.

Another claim, she knew. Like the rings he'd put on her hand today. Like the title he'd bestowed upon her, the throne they now shared, the palace that was to be her home.

He had never looked more like a predator than he did then, the lanterns throwing odd shapes onto the walls of fabric all around them. He was stone and hawk, carved from granite and cast in metal.

And the way he looked at her broke her heart.

Tarek moved to wipe moisture from beneath her eyes. He used his thumbs, touching her carefully, but there was nothing gentle in the expression on his face.

Something inside her rolled over hard, then sank.

"That is a pleasurable duty," he said, horribly. Deliberately. "But it is a duty, Anya. Everything I do, everything I am, is that duty. Sex to me is about succession before it is anything else."

"Succession…" she repeated.

But she was winded. She could feel it as if he'd reached in, scraped her raw, and then sucked everything she was out.

And in return, what was left was that familiar knot in her chest.

It swelled, then pulsed.

"You are a doctor," he said in the same darkly calm way. Still lodged deep inside her, his shoulders wide enough to block the light, as if he'd taken over the whole world. As if he *was* the whole world. "Surely you must have noticed that we have never used anything that might prevent nature from taking its course."

And Anya's brain…blanked out at that, more or less. Still, she heard him. She knew that he was talking about birth control and that she ought to have thought about it.

Why hadn't she thought about it?

Because she hadn't. It had been a month, she was indeed a doctor, and she had never even raised the subject in her own mind. No matter how many times they came together like this. No matter how many times she'd felt him flood her with his release.

Why haven't I thought about it? she demanded silently.

But no answers presented themselves.

There was a curious look on his hard face. "You look so shocked. I assumed it was what you wanted. You surely knew, and when you did not raise the topic, neither did I."

She couldn't quite catch her breath. Or move. "Why would you…?"

"I told you I wanted to marry you." He did something with his jaw that might as well have been a shrug, though there was nothing careless in it. "I am not a man of half measures. Of course if I wished to marry you, that would mean children to follow. You can tell me that you did not know this, if you like. But between you and me, *wife*, I don't believe it."

And there was a truth in his words that she didn't like. Especially not now, when she felt as if he had stripped her of everything, leaving her with nothing.

Nothing but that terrible knot that seemed to grow twice its size in a moment. Then three times its size in the next.

Worse, it hurt.

"You told me I could have whatever I wanted. You promised that no matter what it was, you would make it happen." She shook her head, horrified when she felt tears spill over, but completely unable to do anything but let them. "What do you call this?"

"Practicality," he said, there against her mouth, a bitter kiss. "We can none of us be anything but what we are, Anya. Remember that. It will save you pain."

Then he was moving. Anya struggled to sit up, some part of her thinking she ought to leap to her feet, chase after him, *do* something.

But she couldn't seem to move.

"What if I'm not practical?" she demanded of him as he stood there beside the bed. "Will you throw me back into your dungeon? It is called the Queen's Cell, after all."

"Now I know why," he threw back at her. "You

decide if you want to be my Queen or you wish to be my curse, *habibti*. And I will respond in kind."

And then she watched, in shocked disbelief, as he left her.

On their wedding night.

When he had just finished telling her how little she truly meant to him.

She stayed where she was, trying to breathe. Trying to think of how best to keep fighting—

Until she heard the sound of a motor turning over outside, and she understood.

He wasn't simply leaving the room. He was leaving, full stop.

The message was clear. As long as she insisted on loving him, there could be no stopping him.

When the panic attack hit her that time, she honestly thought that it might kill her. Or maybe she wished it would, this time.

It came on all fronts, walloping her again and again.

She couldn't catch her breath. Her heart pounded so hard it frightened her. She was nauseated. Sweating. Hot, then cold. Then *this close* to bursting out of her skin—

And all the while the tent spun around and around and around, until she was so dizzy she was afraid she might fall down.

It took her a long while to realize that she was already lying flat.

Slowly, laboriously, she pulled herself up, but

she couldn't stand. On and on it went, as if she was caught on some sort of horrid carnival ride. Eventually she made to the side of the wide bed, then to the floor, crawling on her hands and knees across priceless rugs, sure she would die there. Any moment.

There were too many things in her head. The certainty that this time, she really was going to die. That she'd minimized these attacks, called them *panic*, but this would be the end of her. Left behind in her wedding dress, on her hands and knees on the floor of a tent in a desert that even her emotionally vacant father had warned her she'd only chosen to stay in because something was terribly, terribly wrong with her.

She was sobbing or she was gagging, or it was both at once. But still, Anya crawled until she found the bathroom.

And then she celebrated her first night as Queen of Alzalam by curling up in a wretched ball next to yet another toilet, waiting for this violent death to claim her once and for all.

Which gave her ample time to think about all the things that Tarek had thrown at her tonight.

Her love. His horror that she would even use the word. His talk of duty, and her place.

She thought of the Queen's Cell and felt the panic rise all over again as she imagined him throwing her straight back in for another stint of cold stone walls and unyielding iron bars.

Not that it mattered, she thought miserably, there on the floor. Because wasn't this marriage just another kind of prison? Not the way she'd imagined it, but clearly the way Tarek intended.

A sick little repeat of her childhood and the life her mother had left her to, however unwillingly.

Anya already knew where that led.

To this, right here. To that throbbing, blaring knot in her chest and her in a ball on the floor, alone.

And then, through all of that noise and riot, nausea and anguish, she heard a voice as clearly as if someone stood over her.

She blinked, but she was still alone.

"*You are brave, Anya,*" said her mother in her head. In her heart. "*You are fiercer than you know. And you can make your life whatever you want it to be.*"

My life, she thought then. *And certainly my marriage.*

She pulled in a shaky breath, deep. Then let it out, and like magic, the panic disappeared with it.

As if it had never been.

Anya sat up carefully. Gingerly. Waiting for all of those terrible sensations to slam back into her and throw her straight back down into that miserable ball, writhing within reach of yet another toilet.

But it was still…gone.

"*You are the bravest girl I know,*" her mother whispered, deep inside, where Anya understood, then, she always would.

She pressed her hand to that place in the center of her chest, the place where that knot had always blazed at her, and felt her eyes fill anew.

But for a different reason this time.

She'd thought it earlier today, hadn't she? That the panic was her feelings all along. That all those things she'd locked up in her attempt to please her father had only ever waited for her there.

Now she understood that it was more than that.

It had come out medically, because that was the only thing she allowed herself. It had burst forth in symptoms, so she could catalog them. List them. Pretend she could clinically examine her own breakdowns.

Because medicine was the only emotional language she'd ever allowed herself.

But now... Now she knew.

It had been her mother all along, talking to her. Telling her. Showing her by making her stop. By making her listen.

By coming to Anya in the only way she would hear.

She laughed a little bit, there on the floor of a desert tent, still wearing her wedding gown as she crouched there in yet another bathroom.

Because it had worked.

She'd had a panic attack before she chose her specialty in medical school, and knew she wasn't going to choose neurosurgery. She'd another panic attack, a terrible one, the night before she'd taken her medical boards. She'd had them with regularity as a resident. Then, for a time, she'd thought she'd gotten them under control.

Until that last one she'd had while she was still an ER doctor. The one that had made her realize that if she didn't change something, radically, she very well might die of that pressure in her chest.

"Thanks, Mama," she said now, out loud, though her voice was scratchy. "You were pushing me where I needed to go all along."

"*Be brave, Anya,*" her mother had whispered the last time Anya had seen her alive. She'd held her tight, though she'd been so thin by then. So frail. "*I will be with you, always. You only have to look.*"

Anya hadn't looked, but that was okay. Her mother had kept her promise just the same.

She wiped at her face. She took a breath.

And she knew, with a new sort of certainty that reached deep into every last part of her, that she was not going to have a panic attack again. Not ever again.

Because she'd finally cracked the code.

It was love. And who had ever said that love had to be all soft plush toys, big eyes and faint trembling? Anya loved a king who happened to also be a hard man, made of this desert in its formidable starkness.

Loving a man like Tarek was a challenge. Even a calling.

Her calling, she knew, without a shred of doubt.

And this time, Anya was choosing a calling because of love. Because her blood moved hot inside her and she had never felt so much all at once without it flattening her on cold, impersonal bathroom floors. Because she didn't fear him, she loved him, and that meant she could take whatever came. No matter what it was.

Even if what came for them was him.

She was not a soft and trembling thing herself, and that was why he'd chosen her. Tarek could say what he liked about practicality and duty and all the rest. But he'd chosen her all the same.

Just as Anya had chosen him. Because he was absolutely right. She hadn't spared a thought to the possibility they might make a child, and that was so unlike her it really should have been funny.

All along, no matter what they pretended—to themselves and each other—the two of them had been choosing each other.

Anya simply knew it. It was in her now, part of her DNA. And she could have stayed where she was, reveling in this new knowledge, but there was no time for that.

Because Tarek had given her golden opportunity to prove that she was truly his Queen. That she was deserving of the title, and that he might give her anything she wanted, but she would do better in return. She would give him what he needed.

If she had to walk all the way back to the palace, she would.

She staggered to her feet and wandered through

room after room of this marvelous, plush palace that was something far more than a *tent*. She found the entrance and pushed her way out, stopping outside when the beauty of the oasis hit her.

The canopy of stars. The soft lights that showed her date trees dancing in the breeze, and set to glowing all the glorious pools set into the sand.

But most beautiful by far was the figure she saw standing near the water, looking into the indigo depths as if tortured.

Anya glanced to the side and saw a jeep pulled up beneath the palms. When she had been so sure he'd driven it off. That he'd left her here.

Because that was something, she realized, her father would do without a second thought.

And she decided, then and there. This was not her childhood. She was not that daughter her father had ignored—and she was not her mother, either.

Tarek was her husband. This was her marriage.

And Anya was brave. She was fierce. She would make their lives exactly what she wanted.

All she had to do was be the Queen he had chosen her to be, at last.

CHAPTER TWELVE

TAREK STOOD BY the ancient pools, looking for wisdom in the water that men of his blood had long called holy, but seeing only himself.

And the monster he had become.

He despised weakness, and yet it had taken hold of him. It had eaten away at him, leaving nothing behind but the hunger he could no more control than he could feed enough to sate himself.

Making it impossible for him to leave tonight, when he knew that's what he should have done.

To prove to her that what he said was true.

That there was nothing between them but duty. Because that was all that *should* have been between them.

He heard the rustle of her dress first, sounding like the desert breeze. Like the date palms that danced overhead.

And then she was there beside him, reflecting back at him from the water's surface. Tarek turned to look at her, expecting to find her in pieces and already kicking himself for breaking her, no matter how necessary.

But his heart did the kicking, hard against his ribs, because this was Anya. She did not look broken in the least.

"I did not expect you to come after me," he said. When he could.

"Why?" Her tone was arch, and she did nothing to conceal the evidence that she'd been crying from him. She stood beside him as if it was her place, her right, and made him wonder why he thought she should conceal anything. "Because women of your acquaintance are more likely to fling themselves on the mercy of foreign countries than confront you personally? I apologize. I never did learn how to cower."

He admired her, and that was only one of the problems. That was only one of the ways she was tearing him apart, and all she was doing was standing there, watching him calmly.

As if she could see straight through him.

And had every intention of doing it forever.

Something in Tarek…broke.

It was not the duties and responsibilities that marked his life. It had not been the losses he suffered. His mother when he was twelve. His father last year. Worse still, the brother he had loved unconditionally, until the night he'd come to kill Tarek. And had laughed while he'd tried, betraying not only Tarek in that moment, but all of Tarek's memories of their childhood.

As if Rafiq had died that night and killed Tarek, too. Yet both of them had to live with it.

He had survived all of those things, if perhaps more scarred and furious than the cheerful boy he'd been once. He'd had no choice but to survive.

But he didn't know how he was meant to survive this.

It was this. It was her.

It was this woman he never should have met in the first place.

And it was something about being here, far away from the civilization of the city, the dampening influence of the palace, where he could never forget for a moment that he was the King. And what, therefore, he owed everyone around him, all the time.

But out here in the desert, he was only…a man.

With her he became the things he should not whether he wished it or did not.

With her he broke into pieces when he could not break. He tore open, when he needed to remain contained. Himself above all.

"*A broken man can rule, but only ever badly,*" his mother had always told him. Well did Tarek know it. The history of the world was littered with broken men who ruled their countries straight into the dark.

He had always intended to find the light. Always.

"You knew the rules going in," he heard himself say, louder than he could recall ever speaking before. As if he howled to the moon and stars above. "You knew what this was."

"But rules are not who we are," Anya replied, with that impenetrable calm he found a challenge. More than a challenge—it bordered on an assault.

"Rules are what separate us from the beasts," he thundered at her. "And emotions are what separate kings from mere men. I have a country I must think of, Anya. Do you not understand this? I cannot have *feelings*."

Because that was what this was. He understood that now.

He had become the thing he'd sworn he never would.

All because of her. The woman who stood beside him, when he had never wanted that. He thought of that soft, inconsequential girl he had been betrothed to and knew full well that none of this would have happened, had she done her duty. He would have felt nothing. He would have married her, even bedded her, with courtesy and distance. He would have treated her with respect.

He never would have felt a thing.

And now, instead, Tarek felt everything.

Every star in the sky above him was bright and hot and still dull compared to what shined in him now, all because of this woman.

Anya turned to him then, looking at him straight on the way she always did. Direct, to the point.

Honest, something in him whispered.

Neither hiding the emotion he could see on her face nor flinging it at him.

And a great deal as if she was daring him to do the same.

Daring *him*, when no one else would brave such an endeavor.

"I understand," she said, so evenly he had the mad urge to *force her* to sound as uneven as he felt. As messy. As ruined. "If it was easy to fall in love, Tarek, we wouldn't call it falling, would we? If it wasn't overwhelming, we might say we stepped into it. Or slid into it, maybe. But everyone knows falling can only end one of two ways. Either you stick the landing or you don't, and either way, it's probably going to hurt."

That word echoed in his chest. In his head. It beat in him like a pulse.

Like a drum.

"I have spent my life in service to this country," he threw at her. Then his hands were on her again, somehow, holding her close. The look in her eyes was killing him. *She* was killing him, as surely as if she wielded a sword or gun. When all she was doing was looking back at him as if she already knew all the noise and clamor inside of him. As if she heard that same drum. "My entire life, everything I have learned and everything I became, I've done so to better serve and rule this kingdom. And not merely rule from afar, as so many do. I put my body into the fires of war to protect my people. I always will. This is who I am."

"Of course it is," she said softly. "No one doubts you are a great king, Tarek. How could they?"

"What you're asking me to do is—"

But he couldn't finish.

And all the while the drums grew louder.

"I'm asking you to love me," Anya said, but she didn't sound anguished. She sounded resolute. "I'm asking you to let me love you. I'm asking you to let us build a family, but not because it's our duty. Not only because of that and not only because we intend to raise them in your family's tradition, but because we want them to really understand what a family is."

"Anya…" he gritted out.

"You're right that I never mentioned protection," she said, and to his astonishment, she smiled. How could she *smile* when he was being torn asunder where he stood? "I didn't even think of it and I used to give lectures on the topic. How could I possibly have failed to think about something so important?"

She shook her head, still smiling. Still wrecking him without even seeming to try.

Tarek tried to gather himself, but it was no use.

"I'll tell you why," Anya continued. "Despite some reports, I didn't lose my mind in that cell. If anything, it clarified my life for me. And then there you were, with your hand outstretched, and I knew."

He shook his head at that as if he could ward it off—push her away—but even as he did, he held her close.

"I couldn't admit it to myself," she told him. "I

didn't have the words. But I knew, Tarek. And I think that every choice I made that day was in service to this. *Us.* To building the family we were always meant to be."

"Anya. *Habibti.*"

But she didn't stop. "I don't want a family like the one I already have, Tarek. I don't want the coldness, the contempt. I think it's possible that my father knew how to love a long time ago, but I don't think it's in him any longer. I don't ever want a child of mine to feel the way that I have, all these years. And I don't believe that the man you are—the King you are—would tolerate treating his own child the way you saw my father treat me. You leaped to my defense. How could you visit that upon your own?"

He didn't understand what was happening in him. The earthquake that was ripping him open when he could see that the palms behind her stood tall.

"My mother warned against this," he managed to get out. "She was never involved in the harem's squabbles, because she wasn't emotional. She thought that it made her a better queen that she did not love my father and I have always agreed. The less emotion, the better. But I neglected to guard against other kinds of love. I was reckless enough to love my brother so blindly I overlooked his flaws, and nearly died for that folly. I want no more emotion in my life, Anya. None."

"Your brother is a coward and a snake. He's precisely where he belongs, and you put him there. And loved him enough to let him live."

"It was an act of mercy, nothing more."

"Tarek. What is mercy if not love?"

He wanted to shout at her. He wanted to shout down the trees. He wanted to wrestle the stars, and beat them into darkness—but all he could do was stand there as this woman tore him apart.

"And maybe not loving her husband did make your mother a better queen." Anya held his gaze. "Maybe that was exactly what your father needed. But Tarek. Do you think I don't know who *you* are?"

And Tarek was a man who had always known who he was. From the day of his birth, his destiny was secure. He had never had a moment's doubt, never suffered from the trials of insecurity. How could he?

He knew who he was. What he was. What he would do, how he would do it, and how history would record him.

He had always known.

Now he gazed down at this woman, his wife and his Queen, who made his heart beat. Who made him want things he'd never considered possible or even desirable before.

And it suddenly became critical to him that he know who *she* thought he was.

"You don't need a cold queen, or a harem filled with women, none of whom love you so much as they love power," she told him when he didn't answer her question. Because he couldn't. "You need me and you know it."

And for perhaps the first time in his life, Tarek found himself appreciating the power of pure confidence in another. Because Anya wasn't asking him or begging him, she was telling him.

She kept going. "You would never have chosen a prisoner and elevated her as you did otherwise. You would never have defended me against my own father, in public. Or left me with your own family the way you did, with no worries whatever that I might embarrass you or act against you in some way. You need me, Tarek. The woman who loves you. The Queen who will defend you."

"Anya." And her name was that drumming thing, and that drumming was a song. He could hear it in the night all around them. In the wind and the sand. In him and between them. And, at last, Tarek stopped fighting it. "I fear…that want to though I might, I do not know how to love."

And her smile then was so bright it made the heavens dim.

"Then I will love you enough that you are forced to learn," she whispered.

This time, when Tarek broke, he understood it was nothing to fight. It was no surrender. It was no rebellion he needed to quell.

Unless he was very much mistaken…this was falling.

And she was right. It hurt.

But that hardly mattered. What was one more scar to add to his collection?

"And if I already love you," he managed to ask, though his heart ached. His temples were spikes of pain. He fell and he fell. "What then?"

Anya slid her arms around his waist, and tilted her head back to look him full in the face. "We will make our own rules, here and now. You and I. We can do as we like, Tarek. This is ours."

And he thought, then, of possibilities instead of problems. Of hope instead of tradition.

Of love—not instead of duty, but laced through it, making it glow.

He thought, *Have I loved her all along?*

And the thought itself seemed to fuse with that smile on her face, the stars all around them, and all the ways he fell. Until he was filled with a wild sense of wonder.

"I think I stuck the landing, *habibti*," he told her, and his reward was not only the way her smile widened and took the world with it. But the way it felt inside him, a wild rush that left him smiling, too.

"I love your scars, that you won in defending this kingdom even though it broke your heart," she said, moving her hands lightly over his chest, tracing one scar. Then the next. He felt it like light, though he still wore his robes. "I love your arrogance and your certainty, because it makes it so evident that you could never be anything but a king. I love my King, Tarek."

He wanted to speak, then, but he was filled with that wonder and a bright, almost painful *thing*—

It occurred to him, at last, that it had never been obsession.

This was so much more than that. *She* was.

"And you deserve to love me back, King and man alike," she whispered fiercely. "You deserve a place where you can hide, Tarek. Where you can be who you are. No thrones or kingdoms or worries. No people. Just you and me. Just this."

Tarek felt washed clean. Made new. He held her face between his hands again, but this time there was no darkness in it.

Because there was none left in him.

For she was a light far brighter than the desert sun, and he could feel her inside him like the brightest, hottest midday.

"Just as you deserve a place where you can shine, Anya," he told her gruffly. "Queen always. *My* Queen, always. And whatever you want of me, you will have, as long as I draw breath."

"Tarek," Anya whispered. "I do love you. So much."

"I love you," he whispered back, because there was no other way to describe the tumult. The longing and the light. The fury and the fear. The endless need, the sharp joy.

Her. Anya.

It was falling and then falling more. It was a tumble from a height so high it made his whole body seize—

But the landing was worth the fall.

It was the way she smiled at him. It was the ferocity in her voice when she came to find him, wherever he'd gone. It was the way she'd knelt before him on a terrace long ago, taking him deep in her mouth and absolving him of the scars he wore, the wars he'd won.

It was the love in her eyes, then and now. Always.

"I love you," he said again, because it barely scratched the surface. It was too small a word, and yet it was everything.

"Tarek," she whispered. "I love you, too."

"Teach me how to love you," he demanded, urgently. "Teach me every day. And I promise you, Anya, I will give you the world."

She slid her hands up the length of his chest, then looped her arms around his neck. And then they were both falling, together, and that was no less overwhelming, but it was theirs.

This was all theirs.

And it was good. And Tarek intended to keep on falling, forever.

He was the King of Alzalam, and he would see to it personally.

"Don't you see?" Anya asked, breathlessly, still smiling as if she would never stop. "You already have."

And later, Tarek thought, he would think of that

scene by the pools as the real moment they became husband and wife, man and woman.

Them.

Forever.

But here and now, he stopped wasting time, and kissed her.

CHAPTER THIRTEEN

TEN YEARS LATER, Anya waited for her husband near
the pools at the oasis, on a night so like their wedding night that she found she couldn't stop smiling.

This time, she wore a shift dress and little else,
sitting on a rock with her feet in the silky water. No
bulky wedding gown that had required both of them
to remove.

Eventually.

They had kept their promises to each other. There
had been press releases and publicity tours, but that
fell under the mantle of *duty*. They were both deeply
dedicated to doing their duty.

But when they were alone, they were something
more than a king and a queen, the embodiment of a
kingdom's hopes and dreams.

They made their own hopes and dreams, together.

He told her stories of Rafiq and the childhood
they'd shared, learning how to grieve what was lost
without letting what had happened tarnish the good
that had happened first. And because he'd trusted

her with that, she told him about her panic attacks and her mother, and how she was reclaiming her own memories of the happy life she'd had when her mother was alive.

Because grief was love. And because they were together, there was no need to fear love, no matter how it presented itself.

Loving each other was the best antidote to fear that Anya could have imagined.

And it only grew with time.

Anya gave birth to Crown Prince Hakim before their first anniversary. She stood beside Tarek on the balcony called the King's Overlook where he'd taken her to announce their engagement, showing off the next generation to the crowds below.

"*You look so happy*," she'd whispered, brought nearly to tears at the sight of this tiny creature they'd made tucked up safe and sound in his father's arms. And she didn't think it was entirely due to her new mother hormones, either.

It was him.

Tarek had turned to smile at her—the smile that was only for her, no matter where they happened to be.

"*I have long dreamed of this moment*," he'd told her. "*But I find that now it is here, what I care about is you, by my side. My Queen outside these walls. My wife within. But most of all, mine.*"

"*Yours*," she'd agreed. "*Always yours.*"

They'd made two more princes to keep Hakim

company, then a brace of princesses. Each and every one of them a perfect bundle of dark eyes, dark hair, and a deep stubbornness they took pleasure in claiming came from the other.

"*Behold your work*," Tarek had said one morning in the great courtyard, years back, shaking his head as his firstborn son and heir ran in circles. Naked. "*This is the future of my kingdom.*"

Anya had only laughed.

"*That sounds familiar, doesn't it*?" she'd asked him one afternoon, years later, when their tiny, perfect eldest daughter was found in one of the palace's public rooms.

And refused to leave.

"*No*," she kept saying. "*No*."

With all the consequence of a king.

Tarek had laughed too, but he'd also pulled Anya close and kissed her soundly.

They tended to their duties, they were deeply involved in the raising of their children, and at night they repaired to the King's royal suite and set themselves on fire.

Over and over and over again.

Year after year. Whether Anya was big with child or not. Whether they had fought for days or not.

They might not have always agreed with each other. They might have spent hours shouting. She was too direct and he was too arrogant and sometimes those things left bruises no matter how much they loved each other.

But they kissed each other's wounds, there in the dark of their big, wide bed. And when he moved inside her and she clung tight to him, they found their way back to each other. Sooner or later, they always found their way.

As the years passed, Tarek became a powerful new voice in the region. And Anya found ways to use the power he'd given her to truly do her best to make the world a better place. She and her sister-in-law Nur first became friends, then partners in a charitable initiative that promoted women's health and wellness.

"*Finally,*" she told Tarek at the charity's inaugural ball. "*A use for all my medical knowledge.*"

"*You will always be my doctor, habibti,*" he'd told her, there in the center of the ballroom where his gaze told her what his hands and his mouth would, later. When they were alone and naked and making each other fall all over again.

Anya thought of her mother daily and never did have another panic attack, as she'd known she wouldn't. Instead, she pursued the dreams of that long-ago little girl. She danced often, because she was a queen and her husband was a king and there were an endless array of balls for them to attend. She had tried painting things as a hobby, but had found herself both terrible and bored.

Her true artistic genius was still in the medium of crayons, in her opinion—something she discovered by coloring things with her children and then festooning them about the bedroom for Tarek to find. Then find creative ways to both laugh at her and praise her at the same time.

Usually he chose to take her flying, without wings or a plane, as only he could.

The most surprising twist had happened back in Seattle. Charisma had left Alzalam a new woman. She had stopped fluttering and had laid down a series of ultimatums, the crux of which was that she no longer intended to be a lapdog of any kind.

Anya's father and his latest, youngest wife were still together, ten years later. With twins Preston doted on.

"Part of me wishes he could have been a better father to me," Anya had confessed to Tarek one night, after one of her father and Charisma's annual visits—something else her stepmother had insisted on. *"But if he had, would I be here now?"*

"That almost makes me like him," Tarek had growled.

She and her father were not close. He had never apologized and never would. She didn't understand him and never would. But they tried, in their way. And she and Charisma had become friends out of the bargain.

It was hard to imagine a better outcome.

And now a whole decade had passed, laced with its own share of disappointments, certainly. But brighter with hope, all the same. Stronger by far for the tests they'd faced along the way.

"Life is good, Mama," Anya whispered into the night. "Life is so good."

She heard Tarek come out of the tent, then. They liked to come here whenever they could, but that didn't mean he could always leave the palace behind. After their long, leisurely dinner in that bright and sprawling room where he'd once tried to put her in her place, he'd taken an urgent phone call.

Anya had checked in with the children and their nannies, had taken care of a pressing matter with her own doctor, and had come outside to wait for him.

She tilted her head, listening to the cadence of Tarek's voice and ready to be what he needed when he came to her. Sometimes he raged. Sometimes he grieved. Now and again he was lost.

He came to her as he was, however he was, and she held him. She challenged him. She was strong for her King and when he could be a man again, he was always hers.

Always and ever hers.

Tonight he sounded good. And then he ended the call and she heard him walk toward her.

And wasn't at all surprised when he simply lifted her up, turning her so he could hold her in his arms.

"Happy anniversary, my love," he said in a low voice, there against her mouth.

"Only a decade," Anya replied. "It seems like a week. And forever."

Tarek kissed her as he always did. As if it was the first time, desperate and needy.

And when she was panting against his mouth, he smiled. "Well?"

She laughed. "Why do you ask when you already know? You always know before I do."

Tarek moved back, then went to his knees before her. This big, strong man. This powerful King.

He slid his hands over her belly and kissed her there. Then grinned up at her.

"Every centimeter of you is precious, and mine," he said with all the dark arrogance she adored. "I know when something changes."

"Yes, I'm pregnant again," she said. "The doctor just confirmed it. But you knew that."

"I did." His grin faded, and something stark replaced it. Stark like the desert all around them, beautiful and vast. "You keep teaching me that no matter how much I love, there is always more. There is no end to it."

"There is never any end," she agreed, her eyes getting glassy. "Not as long as we're together."

Tarek stood them. He bent to scoop her into his arms and then he held her there, gazing down at her.

"Come, *habibti*," he said, the way he always did. The way he always would. "Let us fall the rest of the way together."

And then he carried her off into the night, falling sweetly into the rest of their beautiful lives.

* * * * *

Captivated by Chosen for His Desert Throne?
Find your next page-turner with these other
Caitlin Crews stories!

His Scandalous Christmas Princess
Christmas in the King's Bed
Claimed in the Italian's Castle
The Italian's Pregnant Cinderella

Available now!

WE HOPE YOU ENJOYED
THIS BOOK FROM

Escape to exotic locations where passion knows no bounds.

Welcome to the glamorous lives of royals and billionaires, where passion knows no bounds. Be swept into a world of luxury, wealth and exotic locations.

8 NEW BOOKS AVAILABLE EVERY MONTH!

#3885 AFTER THE BILLIONAIRE'S WEDDING VOWS...
by Lucy Monroe

Greek tycoon Andros's whirlwind romance with Polly started white-hot. Five years later, the walls he's built threaten to push her away forever! With his marriage on the line, Andros must win back his wife. Their passion still burns bright, but can it break down their barriers?

#3886 FORBIDDEN HAWAIIAN NIGHTS
Secrets of the Stowe Family
by Cathy Williams

Max Stowe is commanding and completely off-limits as Mia Kaiwi's temporary boss! But there's no escape from temptation working so closely together... Dare she explore their connection for a few scorching nights?

#3887 THE PLAYBOY PRINCE OF SCANDAL
The Acostas!
by Susan Stephens

Prince Cesar will never forgive polo star Sofia Acosta for the article branding him a playboy! But to avoid further scandal he must invite her to his lavish banquet in Rome. Where he's confronted by her unexpected apology and their *very* obvious electricity!

#3888 THE MAN SHE SHOULD HAVE MARRIED
by Louise Fuller

Famed movie director Farlan has come a long way from the penniless boy whose ring Nia rejected. But their surprise reunion proves there's one thing he'll never be able to relinquish...their dangerously electric connection!

YOU CAN FIND MORE INFORMATION ON UPCOMING HARLEQUIN TITLES, FREE EXCERPTS AND MORE AT HARLEQUIN.COM.

HPCNMRB0121

"Mr. Alexandris," Tansy pronounced rather stiffly.

"Come sit down," he invited lazily. "Tea or coffee?"

"Coffee please," Tansy said, following him around a sectional room divider into a rather more intimate space furnished with sumptuous sofas and then sinking down into the comfortable depths of one, her tense spine rigorously protesting that amount of relaxation.

She was fighting to get a grip on her composure again but nothing about Jude Alexandris in the flesh matched the formal online images she had viewed. He wasn't wearing a sharply cut business suit—he was wearing faded, ripped and worn jeans that outlined long, powerful thighs and narrow hips and accentuated the prowling natural grace of his every movement. An equally casual dark gray cotton top complemented the jeans. One sleeve was partially pushed up to reveal a strong brown forearm and a small tattoo that appeared to be printed letters of some sort. His garb reminded her that although he might be older than her, he was still only in his late twenties, and that unlike her, he had felt no need to dress to impress.

Her pride stung at the knowledge that she was little more than a commodity on Alexandris's terms. Either he would choose her or he wouldn't. She had put herself on the market to be bought, though, she thought with sudden self-loathing. How could she blame Jude Alexandris for her stepfather's use of virtual blackmail to get her agreement? Everything she was doing was for Posy, she reminded herself squarely, and the end would justify the means…wouldn't it?

"So…" Tansy remarked in a stilted tone because she was determined not to sit there acting like the powerless person she knew herself to be in his presence. "You require a fake wife…"

Jude shifted a broad shoulder in a very slight shrug. "Only we would know it was fake. It would have to seem real to everyone else from the start to the very end," he advanced calmly. "Everything between us would have to remain confidential."

"I'm not a gossip, Mr. Alexandris." In fact, Tansy almost laughed at the idea of even having anyone close enough to confide in, because she had left her friends behind at university, and certainly none of them had seemed to understand her decision to make herself responsible for her baby sister rather than return to the freedom of student life.

"I trust no one," Jude countered without apology. "You would be legally required to sign a nondisclosure agreement before I married you."

"Understood. My stepfather explained that to me," Tansy acknowledged, her attention reluctantly drawn to his careless sprawl on the sofa opposite, the long, muscular line of a masculine thigh straining against well-washed denim. Her head tipped back, her color rising as she made herself look at his face instead, encountering glittering dark eyes that made the breath hitch in her throat.

"I find you attractive, too," Jude Alexandris murmured as though she had spoken.

"I don't know what you're talking about," Tansy protested, the faint pink in her cheeks heating exponentially. Her stomach flipped while she wondered if she truly could be read that easily by a man.

"For this to work, we would need that physical attraction. Nobody is likely to be fooled by two strangers pretending what they don't feel, least of all my family, some of whom are shrewd judges of character."

Tansy had paled. "Why would we need attraction? I assumed this was to be a marriage on paper, nothing more."

"Then you assumed wrong," Jude told her without skipping a beat.

Don't miss
The Greek's Convenient Cinderella
available February 2021 wherever
Harlequin Presents books and ebooks are sold.

Harlequin.com

HPEXP0121

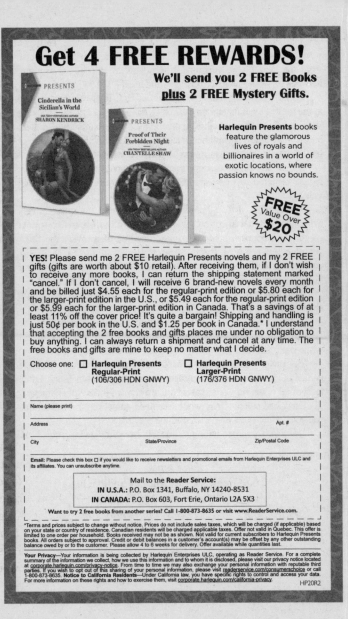